Threads of THE WAR

Threads

of

THE WAR

Personal Truth-Inspired Flash-Fiction of *The 20th Century's War*

A Collection of Historical Short Stories by:

JEREMY STROZER

Threads of The War

By Jeremy Strozer

Published by The Good Enough Empire, LLC.

Falls Church, VA 22043 USA

Jeremy Strozer
Print Edition
ISBN-13: 978-0-692-79428-9

In cherished memory of Sharon Colen <u>and</u> Laura
Flint. A loving mother

Contents

Acknowledgments..1

Introduction 5

Above the Din 9

Couples Retreat...21

Big-Dog Fight..27

Old Dogs...39

The March 45

PTLPTA 51

The Imperial 59

Tondelayo 79

Slavery...85

Nishi 91

Tank vs. Battleship 99

Enemy Honor 105

Over the Top 138

The Offer 150

Boise City..158

Flatcar 168

First Line of Defense 176

Afterword..186

About the Author 190

Acknowledgments

This book would not exist without the loving support of my wife, Jan Strozer, who through every up and down, always believed in me. Throughout the years of writing and reviewing, my mother-in-law (Jan's mom), Linda Stennett, provided immeasurable feedback; without which I could not imagine having written more than a few stories. Joshua Strozer, my son, inspired me to think through war's costs and consequences; allowing me to hope that my work may help contribute to fewer of them, and a better chance that he will not be called to serve in one.

A special place of gratitude is held in reserve for my moms, Laura and Kathy Flint, who had set as their mission to keep me from war, even to the point of intimidating the West Point recruiter so he never called upon our home again.

Without my father's affinity for military equipment and his own understanding of history and politics, I may never have found my niche and attraction to history.

My short mission to Vietnam, sponsored by Pat Patierno through the Weapons Removal and Abatement Office of the United States Department of State, opened my eyes to the personal cost of war, the enduring legacy of the residue of war, and the power those determined to help have over the destructiveness of decisions made by officials in far-off capitals over the lives of innocents touched by war.

Throughout my life, many people served as mentors, offering their experience and insight into my development as a storyteller and student of history. Each, in their own way contributed to the creation of this work: Eric Flint, Joshua Spero, Sean Kay, Marc Cogen, Alan Strozer, Steven Panzer, Jud Ireland, Teah Strozer, Paula Killian, Scott Whitehair, Nadine Warner, Hal Bidlack, Steven Ball, Shulamit Widawsky, Gary Bratschie, Robert Colton, Stephanie Schwartz, and many others.

A special thanks goes out to the BETA readers whose words of encouragement, and many great edits, brought the life into these stories: Jonathan Benton, John Bernhardson, John Costant, Philip Drayer, Emilio Iasiello, Wesley Ratko, Caitlin Rourk, Richard Saunders, Maggie Teliska, and JD Williams.

Finally, I would like to express a sincere thank you to all of the teachers who believed in me at The George Washington University, Granada Hills High School, Acalanes High School, Sequoia Middle School, Pleasant Hill Elementary, and Pinecrest in Thousand Oaks. At each of these institutions of learning, I found caring professionals who inspired a little boy, then a young man, and ultimately a passionate adult to look at the past, understand its context, and think about what the links between all things mean for the future.

Introduction

History is a collection of personal narratives woven together to form the tapestry of our human story. Within ancient historical texts, we recognize the personal stories told by Homer, Herodotus, and Thucydides as they play out on the page. We know they are perspectives rather than simply facts, which makes them compelling to read and powerful tools from which to learn.

Capturing history from personal narrative draws us into the struggles of the individual, allows us to enter that particular time and place, and can offer us the only true image of inputs leading to world-changing decisions. Stories are our way of connecting to each other through our shared past. Personal stories are a compelling way of experiencing that past, in the present.

War is as old as history. Humans are violent toward each other. Personal experiences in war are most often tragic, occasionally humorous, frequently ironic, sometimes banal, and often present – for those who participated – memories they wish to forget. Warfare draws from us raw emotions, forces us to seek refuge in person as well as mind, shakes our fundamental values, and pushes us to commit acts we could never imagine under any other circumstance. When observed from the outside, war and the actions taken by those in it, are often misunderstood. When experienced from within, war is broken down into minute occurrences from which the human perspective can be shared and learned.

This book is a collection of flash-fictional stories about real events, with individuals experiencing multiple aspects of *The 20ᵗʰ Century's War*. This was a war begun in 1898 with embers still afire today in many parts of the world. Most of these stories are pulled from World War I and World War II, which I consider a single major chapter of *The 20ᵗʰ Century's War*, spanning a period of over thirty years. Considering the scale of that worldwide conflagration, the carnage suffered upon humanity and the Earth, and the personalities involved, no book could possibly do justice to the personal stories of every individual present.

My goal, therefore, is not to be comprehensive, but rather demonstrative, by offering threads of personal trial, triumph, and tragedy. These threads represent the time, people, places, and decisions involved. They are not fact, although all are derived from real incidents. These are fictional accounts of real events meant to offer a glimpse at what may have gone through the minds of those caught up in a global catastrophe in which simply finding a clear path to safety was a momentous achievement. As threads, they are small components of the fabric which weaves into a personal history through war. That fabric of personal history, when woven with the personal history of every other person of that time, creates the tapestry of our human story. May this tapestry entertain, as well as educate.

Above the Din

"**O**k, you ready?"

"Yes, all set."

"All right. I've let go. You are now flying the plane."

My fourteen year-old son sits so close to me in our little Aeronca that his left arm has to brush my right shoulder each time he makes any adjustment to the plane's heading.

We've been in the air for only about fifteen minutes on this trip, our third since he expressed interest in learning to fly like his old man.

Watching him guide this aerial wonder far above the island of Oahu sends shivers down my spine, shivers of pride mixed with longing. Pride at the young man he is becoming; longing for the little boy who used to rely on his mother and me for every aspect of his existence. To be a father is to transform from the existential to the occasionally useful over the course of just a few short years. When did Martin become a being capable of flying a plane? When did I become something other than his dad? Will he still need me in a few more short years?

A warm thrust of air tosses our little flying machine like a toy. Martin adjusts well, returning the Aeronca to level flight quickly. I scan the sky and ground below. We are high over Pearl Harbor on this sleepy Sunday morning. Far below us, naval personnel are preparing for morning services. Launch boats are scattered across the harbor, connecting the ships to shore and bringing back to their berths those sailors who stayed out too late last night.

With a clear view of the horizon, as well as the harbor below, I can see right over the Koolau and Waianae Mountain Ranges at the northern end of the island. What a great day for a flight, for Martin is not yet ready to deal with low visibility. I still have a purpose as long as his field of view is cloudy, a thought that is only slightly reassuring.

"Dad, can we fly out over the water?"

We have enough fuel for two hours of flying time, so there is no reason we can't head out over the water for a little while.

"Sure, would you like to turn?"

"Yes!"

"All right, gently this time."

As Martin slowly and gently banks the plane to the right, my field of vision crosses the mountains north of Pearl Harbor. Glints of reflections pop up at spaced intervals across the horizon throughout our turn.

What could those be? I ask myself, keeping my eyes on them as my head turns away from the direction of the plane's heading.

I am fixated on these glinting objects for as long as it takes me to realize they're coming closer. At first, I cannot make them out until it dawns on me: They're airplanes.

The Army or Navy must have a large flight of aircraft coming in from the North.

Yet, looking down at Ford Island and remembering back at Henderson Field as we took off, I recall seeing what I can only imagine to be the entire air force lined up wingtip to wingtip on those tarmacs.

Where could these planes be coming from?

"Hey, Buddy, let's head east, toward the airfield. We don't have to land yet, but let's stick near the field for now."

Martin is visibly disappointed. He wanted to fly over the water for a while longer. I just don't feel quite right about these planes and cannot take my eyes off of them as they approach ever closer.

"You see those planes out there?"

"Yeah."

"I want to get out of their way. You mind if I take over for a few minutes?"

"Ok," he says grudgingly.

Within those minutes, the planes have visibly multiplied to more than 100.

Where are they all going to land? The air-fields are all so crowded already.

I aim us back toward John Rodgers Airport, which means crossing back over Ford Island on our way.

As we approach the western edge of Ford Island, the planes begin to swarm around us. They're approaching from the north, east, and west. The ones coming from the north and west are on us first. Within seconds, I can see their markings.

"They're Japanese!" I exclaim in a voice that reveals a level of alarm I believe is less than reassuring to Martin.

"Japanese, what are they doing here?"

"I don't know, but we should get out of here!"

The moment the last syllable finishes exiting my mouth a torpedo disconnects from one of the lower flying planes approaching from the East toward the battleships lined up on the Eastern side of Ford Island.

"They're attacking!"

Now I am scared! My son and I are up here in the middle of a Japanese attack!

The Japanese planes swarm past us. Some are high above our heads, from where they begin to drop objects toward the ships below.

Those must be bombs!

Others are flying in low, probably with torpedoes strapped to their bellies, on their way to attack the ships at port.

Clink, Clink, Clink, Clink

"What was that?" Martin asks in a terrified voice as a Japanese plane streaks past us, machine guns blazing for a brief instant before it stops firing.

Shit, he attacked us!

I max out the engine and start to descend to gain as much speed and distance from the Japanese as possible.

A second Japanese fighter screams by us, the pilot clearly visible in the cockpit. He is staring at us

in contemplative disbelief before he heads off to the
North.

Thank God, they realize we're civilian!

A massive explosion erupts in the harbor below.

"Dad, I'm scared!"

"I am too, buddy. We're getting out of here as fast as we can!"

I keep descending, gaining over 50 miles an hour more than when I first started hightailing it out of dodge.

I just have to get us back to the airport!

My son's left arm is now pressed firmly against my right. Even in this already cramped little cockpit, he has found a way to make himself closer to me than either of us would have expected possible.

Most of the Japanese planes are overhead now. A few torpedo planes are still near our altitude, but they're heading into Pearl Harbor, rather than toward John Rodgers.

Another explosion erupts behind us. I don't want to look. Martin doesn't look either.

We are both escaping this scene. A task made easier if we ignore the events taking place directly behind us. Reality and awareness are not always useful, especially when trying to maintain a semblance of composure when hell is breaking loose.

We are getting so close to John Rodgers now.

I just have to make it to the airfield. I just have to make it to the airfield.

A Japanese fighter zips past us, machine guns blazing, as it attacks the Army Air-Corps fighters lined up at Hickam Field.

Another close call.

We're making our approach.

No signals from the tower, no guidance, no flags are visible.

I don't care. I'm going to get us on the ground.

Martin is practically on my lap now he is leaning in so close.

Our wheels touch down.

I quickly lower the throttle to taxi speed and move us off the runway toward a line of bushes along the edge of the grass.

As the plane approaches the bushes, I order Martin "I'm going to kill the engine. Get out and head to the bushes. Once in the bushes, get far away from the plane!"

The engine begins to die down.

"Go now!"

Martin leaps from the plane, running perpendicular to its direction in order to make the bushes quickly.

I kill the engine before leaping out myself.

Within seconds, I run around the plane and catch up with Martin who is working his way through a thicket. He reaches out his hand to me.

I take it as we run together. When we're more than fifty yards from the plane I give a gentle tug. "We'll be good if we crouch here."

A pair of Japanese fighters skims overhead, heading toward the burning planes at Hickam Field.

Martin holds my arm, curling his body within the fold of mine. We are both shaking.

With my left hand, I rub the top of his head.

His face looks hard, missing its boyhood soft innocence.

"You did a good job, buddy. You did a good job."

"So did you Dad."

*****

1940 Aeronca 11AC Chief
https://commons.wikimedia.org/wiki/File:Aer-
onca_11ac_chief_g-ivor_1940_arp.jpg

The first American aircraft to face the Japanese aerial assault on Oahu was a small civilian
plane, an Aeronca 65TC, which was in the air when
the Japanese attack force showed up. While on an
early morning pleasure flight, attorney and future
Territorial Legislator Roy A. Vitousek and his son
Martin were unexpectedly caught in the middle of the
Japanese attack.

The little Aeronca suffered some bullet dam-
age before it was able to land at John Rodgers Airport
(Now Honolulu International Airport) at 8:10 a.m.
Roy and Martin safely exited the aircraft and hid in

the bushes alongside the runway to avoid being strafed.

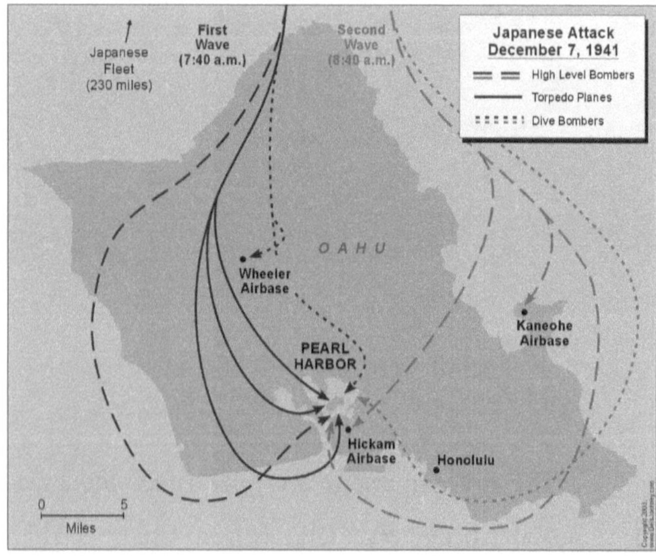

The Japanese attack on Oahu Island, December 7, 1941.
http://www.privatetourshawaii.com/blog/the-bombing-of-pearl-harbor

Couples Retreat

"**I** know they're in here, and I'm going to find them!" the menacing-looking uniformed man in his early 30's blares out as he briskly marches past me into the cinema.

"But Sir," I call out, "It's dark, and you'll disturb everyone while you search!"

He marches on, as if he did not hear a word I said.

Oh, what a scandal this will cause. No customers will want to come to the theater if they think they'll be found out. I must do something!

I run directly behind the soldier, passing him as I head toward the front of the packed theater where over 700 people are watching the Cecil DeMille movie, *The Cheat*.

On my way, I tap the piano player a little too hard with my left hand.

Clearly disturbed, he looks at me, but as soon as he sees me signaling with my hand across my throat for him to stop playing, he understands why I surprised him.

Owning the cinema has certain advantages in times of crisis.

"Ladies and Gentlemen," I call out above the protests of the audience.

I would be unhappy too, but they'll thank me once they hear what I have to tell them.

"Ladies and Gentlemen please listen to me!" my voice projects as far as I can send it.

Most of the audience quiets down enough for me to start talking, if I yell.

"LADIES AND GENTLEMENT, THERE IS A MAN IN UNIFORM HERE LOOKING FOR HIS WIFE AND HER LOVER."

Everyone starts talking at once.

"PLEASE BE QUIET. THE MOVIE WILL RETURN IN A MOMENT!" I plead with the audi-ence. "NOW, PLEASE, ALLOW ME TO SPEAK NORMALLY. To avoid a scandal, anyone here who wishes to leave without being seen can exit through a discreet door here at the back of the theater." I point in the direction of an emergency exit we never use; it leads directly to the dark alley behind the cinema.

At once, couple after couple scrambles in the direction I am pointing.

The movie is still playing.

I direct the piano player to start up again.

Couples are descending the staircase in droves as they head for the exit. Right in front of me, the entire front row of the theater departs.

I would not have thought to sit in front with my mistress.

I look up toward the middle, and it too is emptying out.

Oh, in the middle makes more sense.

The back, the balcony, everything.

Is everyone here cheating? I didn't know there were that many men left in town.

Almost every seat is now empty, and a long line has formed at the back exit of the theater.

My God, they were all cheating.

The solid soldier marches toward the couples piling out of the theater, turning one woman and then another around to find the face of his cheating wife.

Looking back at the seats, I can see seven people remaining where they were before I interrupted the show.

Wow, over 300 couples were afraid to be caught together.

Thank God, I'm not a soldier, and my wife and mistress are both at home, safe from this sort of thing.

*****

An Old-time movie theater with piano.
http://www.perfessorbill.com/sources6.shtml

In 1915, a German magazine published an article about a movie theater proprietor who stood in front of an audience to warn them that a man in uniform had entered the theater to catch his wife and her lover, whom he knew were in the crowd. To avoid scandal, the proprietor pointed out a small, discreet emergency exit. Over 320 couples immediately left the theater in semi-darkness.

The Cheat was a real 1915 Cecil DeMille movie the Germans would have been able to view at the time, for the United States was not yet at war with Germany.

Big-Dog Fight

Frustration permeates through the bomber, made unbearable by bursts of frigid air penetrating the thin, poorly-riveted aluminum skin of this lumbering beast. High above the Atlantic Ocean, in search of a British convoy we know is out here, our flight of four Focke-Wulf 200 Condors is closing in on the fail-safe point – when we will have to head back to safety in France or risk running out of fuel. We are more than six hours out of our base near Bordeaux, my stomach is empty, my hands are freezing, even under the fur-lined gloves, and we may have to return home empty-handed.

As a navigator, bombardier, and part-time gunner, my job on this flight has been relatively easy. We are not the lead plane in our formation, so my navigational duties have been light. Because we have not yet found our target, I have yet to work the bombsight. Luckily, we have not been harassed by any escort carrier-based aircraft, so I have not had to fire the machine gun I man in the nose of the plane since testing it shortly after takeoff.

I cannot warm myself up here, so I let my mind wander back to Thursday night. The soft, warm embrace Danielle and I shared through the night heats me from the inside. I can still feel her supple lips on mine as I left her apartment Friday morning. That sensation stayed with me, palpable on my skin and inhabiting my mind. Closing my eyes, I can see her face staring back at me in the silence of the early morning. She opens her mouth….

The blare of the intercom tears me from my dream.

FOUND THE BASTARDS!

Damn, I'd rather be with Danielle.

It's so cold!

EVERYONE, THIS IS IT!

If only I was still in bed instead of floating over….

HEINRICH, GET OFF YOUR ASS!

I rise from the navigator seat in order to bend myself over the bombsight. As I lean forward, the plane lurches to the right.

ANTI-AIRCRAFT FIRE!

Nothing hits us, but the explosion is close. One of the ships in the convoy appears to be spitting fire in our direction. Every British ship these days carries machine guns and anti-aircraft guns, but this ship is different: the size of a cruiser, it appears to be covered from bow to stern with anti-aircraft guns of all sizes intent on sending me to a watery grave.

They're targeting me. What did I do to deserve this? I don't want to be here. I want to be with Danielle.

Flying over the convoy, the first bomber releases its bombs. I can see the black dots descending from the Condors' belly toward the slow-moving tubs below. Slowly, the bombs fall toward the water and its metal-encased occupants attempting to supply

Allied forces in North Africa. The difference between a hit and a miss here could mean the lives of countless soldiers and airmen there.

A HIT!

Yes, they got one!

Just at that moment, number 2 Condor bursts into flames.

The anti-aircraft cruiser is pouring out fiery lead at a horrific rate.

The plane breaks apart, falling out of the sky in fragments of burning metal. Its altitude was so low that I did not see any parachutes before the debris hit the water.

I slowly peel my eyes away from the wreckage to adjust the bombsight. We are at 2,000 meters, traveling at 220 knots, with winds at 14km/h from East by Southeast. My eyes shut for just a moment.

Danielle…

Her image returns to me for a brief instant, filling my mind with the remnants of her sensation. The feeling of her lips on mine returns.

Now it's our turn. Our aircraft changes direction to fly over the ships. I can make out several potential targets in our flight path. A slow-moving freighter is just about three degrees off our current trajectory.

I yell into the intercom, *"Captain, change angle to 189!"*

DON'T YELL, DAMN IT, HEINRICH!

The plane eases over on the new bearing. We approach the freighter. A shudder shakes the plane again. My target is farther away from the cruiser firing all of those anti-aircraft guns than the other possible targets I could have chosen, but that death-wielding monster is still spewing its fire upon us.

Three seconds until we're over the target.

Two.

One.

I release the bombs, then quickly lift my head from the bombsight.

My job is done.

The captain begins a drastic turn, sharper than I expected, knocking me off balance, and pinning me against the glass window to my left.

ENEMY AIRCRAFT AT 9 O'CLOCK!

Shit!

Must get up.

I didn't see an aircraft carrier....

Still pinned to the window of the Condor, I look to my left. In the distance, a lumbering beast, similar in size to our bomber, inches its way toward us.

No news on my bombs yet. They should be hitting about now.

I try to look back, but we have turned so hard that I cannot see the freighter I targeted. I turn toward the enemy plane again to see it is gaining on us.

What's he doing?

I can't believe he's heading right toward us.

A bomber?

The captain banks the Condor to avoid the enemy aircraft. The shift in angle releases me from the sidewall of the aircraft and allows me to head toward the machine gun in front of me. My right hand catches on one of the grips, which I use to pull myself toward the gun.

The enemy plane, now recognizable as a B-24, is barreling at us and pulling up on our left side.

THEY'RE GOING TO FLY BY!

EVERYONE LIGHT HIM UP!

I'm going to get to use my machine gun against another bomber!

I can't see the plane approach, but the sound of machine guns from my own plane fills the fuselage. The enemy bomber gains on us. Every one of its guns - front, side, top and bottom turret, are lit up. We're outgunned two-to-one.

As the enemy bomber moves in, time slows down. I can make out the faces of the men in the plane; all are intently focused on firing their guns at us. I can see the pilot and co-pilot in the cockpit, both looking over as they fly by. The brown wavy hair of the co-pilot captures my attention. It's the same color as Danielle's hair.

We are firing broadsides like those they used with ancient sailing ships, like at Trafalgar!

The distressingly pained strain of metal ripping, human guttural screams, and shrieking bullets tearing through tempered steel and soft flesh claws its way up the Condor in an agonizing eternal fraction of a second. The B-24 is almost up to where my nose gun can have a crack at it.

I aim for the cockpit, hoping to hit the pilot and co-pilot.

I can't fire.

My brain is telling my hand to fire the machine gun, but my fingers will not respond.

Danielle's hair smelled like lilacs.

CRACK CRACK CRACK CRACK CRACK....

My machine gun remains idle in my hands. My world is now closed-in. Blackness descends on my mind, and all I can see is the beast of a bomber directly in front of me. The ball- and the tail-turrets occupy my whole horizon. Both stream forth with orange bursts of glass-shattering, metal-tearing, bone-crushing lead.

My head goes dark.

My hand goes weak.

A punch in my stomach, followed by another in my right shoulder, and then my left leg. Warmth begins to stream over and through me.

I'm in Danielle's arms.

Redness fills my eyes.

Everything is out of sight now.

I am falling.

The Condor's falling to the sea!

My body crashes against the metal frame which once held the glass nose-canopy of our Condor. Shards of broken glass, still inside the frame, scrape across my skin like uncontrollable razors as my body slides down the front of the plane.

There's no pain here.

A slight fragrance of salt wafts to my nose.

Danielle, we're near the water.

I can feel the gentle warm touch of her lips on mine.

Warmth.

*****

Focke-Wulf FW-200 Condor
© Simon W Atack,

In the summer of 1943, the British were struggling to supply the beleaguered island of Malta in the central Mediterranean. Many times during these missions, German long-range bombers attacked the convoys attempting to progress through the dangerous gauntlet of aircraft, surface ships, and other Axis threats.

On one such occasion, an American B-24 Liberator in the area by chance, pounced on the German aircraft. On the deck of the HMS Scylla, a torpedo officer gave a blow-by-blow account of the duel to the crew below the decks. "The Lib is right on his tail; now he's above him. Hold on a moment, chaps, something's going to happen. It has. Jerry's plunged into the drink."

B-24 Liberator

Old Dogs

"Then get up and show us." Il Duce—Benito Musso-lini—jokes to Foreign Minister Ciano in front of the Fascist Grand Council, Italy's small coterie of leaders.

A smiling Foreign Minister Ciano pushes his chair away from the u-shaped conference table that almost fills the outer edges of the ornately decorated room before he practically waltzes around the corner to take his personally-desired place at the center of attention.

A strong right arm strikes across his breast as his right leg shoots perfectly straight into the air. A moment later, his left leg shoots up, also perfectly straight.

The whole room erupts in laughter.

"No, no, you are doing it all wrong. Do you want to look like a fool?" Mussolini quips, clearly wanting to recapture the room's attention from his son-in-law.

"Il Duce, with all due respect, I was just in Berlin where I witnessed a German army demonstrate it." Ciano replies, demonstrably pride stricken.

"Be that as it may, clearly we all need to learn to goose step properly if we want to look like a professional army," Mussolini rejoins as he shuffles toward the door.

"The Italian people need a marshal inspiration to rally them to greatness!" he shouts while exiting the room.

Where is he going?

"Il Duce!" I call out. "The meeting is over?"

"Yes, Marinelli, we're done here. Everyone outside. We will learn to walk with authority NOW!"

Everyone in the room begins looking around.

The twenty-four of us were summoned here to hear Ciano's tales of the wonders of Hitler's Germany, and now we're going to learn to Goose Step?

De Vecchi and De Bono leap to their feet, followed almost as enthusiastically by the black-shirted Balbo. They quickly follow Il Duce out the door.

40

Everyone else rises a little more slowly than the remaining members of the March on Rome, the once sacred Quadrumvirs.

We all know enough about personal safety not to question Il Duce, even about learning to Goose Step on a cold wet winter day.

I turn to the labor leader, Luciano Gottardi, a small smile across my face.

He smiles back and says, "Looks like we'll need our coats."

All twenty-four of us grab our coats and hats as we make our way down the stairs and out the entryway of the Palazzo di Venezia.

If I'm going to learn to Goose Step on a rainy day, I want to at least be warm and look good doing it.

"Come, come, line up behind ME!" Mussolini belts out, turning his back to the Grand Council members still stumbling out of the Palazzo.

We stand in a long line behind Il Duce. None of us wants to create a second line behind the first; for no one wants to show that he lacks enthusiasm for Mussolini's flights of fancy.

Il Duce spreads his arms to his sides, lifts his right leg straight, and begins marching.

Our arms quickly entangle as each of us, in attempting to simulate the leader's actions, fails to pay attention to the other Grand Council members standing on either side.

I can't kick that high at my age.

Our retinue is gathering attention from the crowds surrounding the Palazzo, with young men and women dashing forth to join the impromptu parade of Fascist leadership.

Soon, Il Duce is leading a several hundred-person procession of goose steppers through the Piazza Venezia toward the stairs of the Altare della Patria.

The crowd is laughing. People are smiling. Il Duce's usually stone face even reveals the slightest hint of a smile, at least for him. His mouth is open.

How brilliant Il Duce is, to have created this mass of support by simply satisfying his momentary flight of fancy.

*****

Benito Mussolini leading the Goose-Step Parade
http://axisandally.tumblr.com/post/43921249989/benito-mussolini-imitating-the-german-goose-step

Benito Mussolini, the fascist dictator of Italy, introduced the goose step in 1938 as the *Passo Romano* ("Roman Step"). He had seen the Germans doing it, and thought it looked marshal. The custom was never popular in Italy's armed forces, only gaining enthusiasm among the Blackshirts, Italy's Fascist diehards.

Less than two years later, another whim of Mussolini's would take an unprepared Italy into World War II. His country would eventually be attacked by both sides and destroyed. Its once mighty leader, Mussolini himself, lost all face before being assassinated and strung up with his mistress from the roof of a gas station to be spit upon by passing pedestrians.

The March

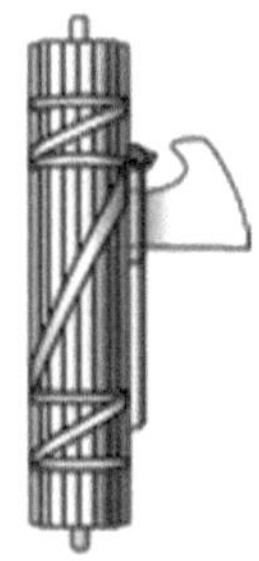

Fasces

Despite the fasces I am holding high in front of me, my view of the processional aisle is clear. When my eyes shift to the left, I can see the Mercedes touring car with the Fuhrer pulling up inside of the stadium. When they shift to the right, I can clearly view Il Duce standing on a platform in the middle of the field. The Leader is surrounded by over 50,000 chanting Fascist Youth. We've been working hard to prepare for the Fuhrer's arrival in our homeland.

I'm so lucky to be here! What a momentous day!

Along with the rest of the crowd, I belt out *Giovinezza* (Youth), our Fascist anthem, as the

Fuhrer steps out of his car. Italy's most imperious young Fascists form an honor guard to greet the Fuhrer. The honor guard marches in Goose Step with the Fuhrer toward The Duce as *Giovinezza* ends, and over 2,500 trumpeters raise their horns in unison. Only a moment of silence punctuates the pause between the marching steps of the Fuhrer before the horns begin to blare a piece from *Lohengrin*, the Fuhrer's favorite opera.

We were told that the trumpeters would play *Lohengrin*, but I am not a horn player, so I did not realize what song was chosen.

Baaa, Bum, Ba, Bum.

This is the "Wedding March!"

The first four notes are all that is required for me to remember going to the opera two years ago with my family and for a small smile to cross my lips.

The Fuhrer marches up to The Leader in time to the even beats of Wagner's wedding song. The Duce stands like a bridegroom awaiting his bride before the altar.

The marriage of Italy and Germany, Europe's Fascist core, will mean great things for the World!

Corrado, who is standing next to me, also holding up a fasces, elbows me in the ribs. He whispers, "I wonder if they're going to exchange rings."

I can't help but laugh. My fasces slips from my hands and falls onto the head of the boy in front of me before falling apart.

That can't be a good omen.

*****

Fascist event at Stadio dei Marmi

In May of 1938, Hitler conducted a whirlwind visit to Italy. Mussolini kept Hitler very busy in his attempt to show how powerful Italy was. He demonstrated the Navy's capabilities and tried to impress Hitler with his organizational and national leadership skill. One event was held at a sports stadium where Hitler was greeted by over 50,000 Fascist Youth who played Hitler the "Wedding March" from *Lohengrin.*

The marriage between The Duce and the Fuhrer turned out very poorly. Italy entered World

War II on the side of Germany in 1940 when it appeared the Germans would win. When the tide started turning in 1943, Italy switched sides and suffered a German invasion. Mussolini was arrested by the new Italian government, but freed through a special operations mission conducted by German forces under Hitler's orders. Mussolini was later captured and killed by Italians.

May this be a lesson to all future bridegrooms. Marriages based on strategic factors alone don't always end well, especially when a poor strategic planner is in charge.

A quick aside between Mussolini and Hitler
http://www.alamy.com/stock-photo/mussolini-hitler.html

http://www.world-war-2-diaries.com/mussolini-biog-
raphy.html

Footage of Hitler's visit to Italy can be seen here:
http://ww2days.com/hitler-pays-state-visit-to-italy-2.html

Color pictures of the visit can be seen here:
http://www.vintag.es/2012/12/hitlers-visit-to-italy-in-
1938.html

A collection of Black-and-White pictures of the
visit can be seen here:
http://www.hitlerpages.com/pagina44.html

PTLPTA

Seventy-eight chairs are always too many, but if we put out any less, there will be too few.

Tearing my eyes away from the always-enthralling lapping waves of the palm tree-lined harbor, I force myself to look over the seven rows of ten chairs, split five to each side of the altar, with a final row at the back of four on either side. I am surprised to find that we seem to be missing two chairs. The storage locker, where the chairs are kept, was locked, but today two chairs appear to have disappeared. Hickam Field, the Naval Air Base at Pearl Harbor, is allocated eighty chairs for regular Sunday outdoor mass.

"Today, we have seventy-eight. It'll have to do, Daniels," I say to the massive seaman helping me set up the chairs before service.

"Yes, Sir," Daniels replies, betraying no sense that because he is the only other person on base with a key to the locker, he may know where the other two chairs went.

As Daniels heads back to the locker to pick up a table, I slip into my vestments before staring down at the Bible upon the altar. Old, sea-worn, faded, and marked on almost every page, this Bible has been with me since I first entered the Navy 30 years ago. A gift from my father as I departed Kansas for training, I've carried it on six continents, 14 Navy ships, and prayed from it at who knows how many services, let alone in my own prayers every morning and night.

My fingers slide over the worn pages as I wait for my flock to arrive for service. The smooth texture of the Bible's hard cover makes an almost grumbling sound as my hands rub across its worn surface.

That grumbling is not the book.

I look up, toward the North, from where the grumbling sound seems to be coming. Just as my eyes cross the peak of the hills just north of Oahu, I see a swarm of planes heading directly toward me.

"Daniels, you see those?" I belt out.

"Meatballs, Sir, they have meatballs on their wings!" he replies, as if he read my mind about what he saw of their markings.

They're Japanese!

"They're Japs! Help me find the gun!"

Before I even finish the sentence, Daniels is racing to the armory with me in close pursuit.

"JAPS, JAPS, JAP PLANES!" Daniels is yelling at the top of his lungs.

Without a second thought to his own safety, Daniels bursts through the armory door, which, while locked, is simply decaying wood and no match for his 210-pound frame.

"I'll take the gun; you get the ammo," I order.

Holding the machine gun in both hands, I flip around before it dawns on me that I'm not sure where I'm going.

I look up to see the Japanese planes barreling over the base, firing at will toward the planes parked wing-tip to wing-tip on the tarmac where they were lined up to defend against sabotage.

Daniels runs past me carrying four cases of ammunition.

I don't think he noticed I stopped. He's probably so used to passing me in a sprint that it did not even occur to him I stopped running.

He heads toward the altar.

Perfect, the altar is a great place to set up the gun!

I dash right after Daniels, hoisting the massive machine gun over my shoulder as I run. My vestments blow in the slight breeze as a Japanese plane rumbles overhead.

Stopping at the altar, Daniels turns to look for me.

I'm right behind him, machine gun on my shoulder. My momentum carries me to the altar, where I slam down the machine gun with a THUD directly atop it.

What a perfect mount!

Daniels starts pulling out a belt of ammunition. I open the top of the gun to load it.

A Japanese plane zeroes in on us, firing its machine guns toward us as we attempt to load the gun.

Rounds spit up the concrete nearby, hurling skyward many of the chairs we had set out for the mass.

Now we'll have to account for even more lost chairs!

"AAAAARRRRRRRRRRGGGGGGGGGGG HHHHHHHHHH" Daniels screams out as a round bursts through his right shoulder, erupting blood and sinew across the altar.

I look at him and then at the half-loaded machine gun.

"I'mmm … o...k." he blurts out, still unloading the ammunition clip from the case with his left hand.

I feed the belt into the machinegun before aiming it toward the closest Jap plane.

ACK ACK ACK ACK ACK ACK ACK ACK ACK

A short burst of fire from our improvised firing platform splashes one Jap.

Daniels looks up at me, a smile on his face.

"WE GOT ONE!" he exclaims.

"PRAISE THE LORD AND PASS THE AMMO!"

Daniels feeds me more rounds, and I keep firing, setting up an arcing barrage as the planes swoop over us.

We're not gonna stop the Jap attack, but at least we'll make 'em pay for disturbing our 8:00 am mass and gettin' blood on my daddy's Bible.

*****

Hickam Field, after the attack
http://www.tampapix.com/tampa1940s6.htm

PRAISE THE LORD AND PASS THE AMMUNITION, as written by Frank Loesser, became a famous song in 1942 from multiple artists including The Merry Macs, The Jubalaires, and in 1943 by Kay Kyser and his orchestra. There are several stories which attempt to claim the origin for this song. Two leading stories are the one above of a Chaplain at Hickam Field breaking into an armory to set up a machine-gun on his altar to fire up at the attacking Japanese aircraft. A second, and the one quoted on Wikipedia, is of Lieutenant Howell Forgy, aboard the USS New Orleans, who inspired the men of his ship to form an ammunition bucket brigade to bring the ammunition up on deck because the ship had no electrical power to use the ammunition elevators to take the rounds up from below decks.

Forgy did not claim the phrase, and it is only attributed to him by the writer Jack McDowall. Chances are there will never be definitive proof of where the phrase came from, but it became an inspiring song for Americans throughout World War II and is quoted in songs, TV shows, and movies to this day.

The Imperial

"*T*his one's playing music," Sanders bellows in the way only a man over 200 pounds can.

"Works for me," Harper pipes up, already opening the door of the seedy-looking skid-row saloon on LA's south side to get out of the pouring rain.

As we cross through the entrance way, one of the two men on stage with guitars calls out "Sail on, sailor boys, sail on! Step up an' give us yer requests!"

Harper looks to Pickett and then at me.

I don't know what to ask for.

"Let's sing 'em one first Woody," the taller guitar player says to his compatriot loud enough for the whole room to hear, "so they'll know it ain't jukebox stuff. What'll we sing? Sailor boys are really wet. Got caught out in the rain."

The other guitar player starts singing in a raspy country voice:

Well, it's rainin' on th' Skid Row

Stormin' down in Birmin'ham

Rainin' on th' Skid Row

Stormin' down in Birmin'ham

But there ain't no stormy weather

Gonna stop these boys of Uncle Sam!

"You tell 'em back there, Cisco!" the other guitar player yells out. "Let 'er reel! Let 'em ramble! Hey! Hey!"

Lord, it's stormy on that ocean

Windy on th' deep blue sea

Boys, it's stormy on the ocean

Windy on th' deep blue sea

I'm gonna bake them Nazis a chicken

Loaded full of TNT!

Turner, my closest friend since we shipped out to California from Great Lakes Naval Base just north of Chicago, calls out to the singers, "Hey, Bud! I ain't got no money, 'cept just a little here to get me a 'burger an' a beer. I'd give you a dime if I had it. But just keep on singing."

Sanders, always a man to go big, yells. "I'm buying, and a round for the entertainment too!"

Both singers smile and keep strumming their chords and chorus as our little group of sailors on leave for the night finishes shuffling into this dive.

"Music! Play, boys, play!" Pickett and Turner grab each other as they begin dancing around the floor. Pickett starts doing the jitterbug while Turner is sticking his fingers up in the air, making all sorts of goofy faces, and yelling, "Yippee! Cut th'rug!"

In some booths opposite the bar, a gaggle of girls is sitting, giggling as they watch Turner and Pickett tear up the dance floor.

Oh, how'd I like to dance with one of them pretty things!

The girls start getting up out of the booths, pairing off with a sailor apiece.

One very pretty young brunette in a blue dress makes her way over to me. "No two men allowed to dance together in this place tonight."

No problem with me!

I smile and reach out my hand.

A blond with curls who took Turner's hand shuffles her feet as she drags a grinning Turner to her "No sailors are allowed to dance unless it's with an awful pretty girl."

Pickett calls out "It never was this a-way back home! Yow!"

Sanders, in the arms of a girl maybe half his size and with a big smile on his face, can't keep his thoughts from spilling out "I hope it stays this a-way fer th' doorashun!"

I call back "Yeah, man!"

On the stage, the two guitar players whip up a version of the old One Dime Blues fast enough to keep up with the jitterbuggers.

Everybody is wheeling and whirling, waving our hands and shuffling along like a gang of circus clowns dancing in the sawdust.

"Mama, don't treat yore daughter mean!" one of the guitar players calls out over the loud speaker.

Answering, the other guitar player sings, "Meanest thing that a man most ever seen!"

My legs are moving, my arms are flailing, my heart is pounding, and little brunette is not only keeping up, her dress is twirling so fast I can almost see the top of her stockings.

What'a night!

The music rolls from the sound holes of the guitars and floats out through the loud speaker so the whole room is pumped with the energy of the singers on stage. The joint is hopping with music and dancing.

Was raining outside. Now dancing with cute girls in this shindig.

Pickett and Turner are bowing their necks, humping their backs, and making goo-goo eyes and clown faces.

Their girls are slinging their hair through the air and spin'n like tops.

"Spin'er, boy!"

"Hey! Hey! I thought I had'er, but she got away!"

Just as we're whooping and hollering, the sound of shattering glass breaks in on our good time.

Something is happening on the street.

The two guitar players stop playing so we can all listen.

People start running past the door, darting around in big bunches, cussing, and hollering.

"Let's go see, boys," Sanders yells as he begins running toward to door.

All us sailors, the girls, and even the guitar players rush outside to see what's goin' on.

"Big fight! Looks like!" Sanders tells us as we enter the street.

Behind me, I hear one of the guitar players say to the other, "Must be a young war!"

We can see a bunch of haggard, dirty lookin' roughs on the other waterlogged curb yellin,' cussin,' and carry'n on.

Turner steps out of our group to walk in front of The Imperial Bar next door. He steps over shards of plate glass from the bar's broken window shattered and strewn across the sidewalk.

Just as he approaches the door of The Imperial, an object flies past his head, smashing a second plate glass window. Sharp shards fly in every direction.

Luckily, no one is hit.

"Who throwed that can of corn?" a lady yells from behind me.

"Was that a can of corn?" one of the guitar players asks.

"Yes. Two cans," she replies. "Who throwed them two cans of corn and broke them windows? I've a good notion to bust my parasol over his head when I find out!"

Sanders is in the street scuffling with one of the roughs.

My little brunette squeezes herself into my side. I wrap my arm around her.

"Don't worry. We won't do nothin' stupid." I say, hoping to soothe her, and my now sharpened nerves.

"You're the man I want, all right!" Sanders gruffly bellows.

"You won't want me very long!" the other guy replies in as gruff a voice.

One of the guitar players announces, "This Imperial Saloon right next door here is run by a whole family of Japanese folks. I know all of them. Sung in there a hundred times. They always help me to get tips. They're just as good as I am!"

He then starts a song on his guitar.

Just as the first notes are making their way to our ears, about ten of the thugs start calling out tough talk in between chews on old cigars and puffs on snipe cigarettes. "We come ta git 'em, an' dam me, we're gonna git 'em! Japs is Japs!"

"I'm da guy wot t'rew dat corn, lady. Whataya gonna do wid me?"

"I'll show you, you big bully!" She waves the can in the air to throw it at him. Right before she releases it, a guy behind her pulls it from her hand.

"No, don't. We don't want to start no trouble. What's this all about anyhow?"

"We're at war with them yeller-belly Japs! An' we come down ta git our share of 'em!" A big man with a scratchy deep, almost lost, voice calls from the curb. "We're 'Meric'ns!"

"You ain't nuthin' but th' worst dam scum of th' Skid Row! Two-bit gambler!" A big half-Indian truck driver calls back as he pushes his way across the street to get the man.

"Jap rats!" another tough one yells out.

"Spies! They tipped off th' Goddam Jap army! These yeller snakes knew to a split second when Pearl Harbor was gonna be blowed up. Git 'em! Jail 'em! Kill 'em!" the rough screams out as he starts crossing the street.

Pickett and Turner start edging their way toward him saying, "You're not going to hurt anybody, Mister Blowoff!"

"Where is th' cops?" little brunette asks me.

I dunno, but don't wanna fight these guys. I was havin' fun.

"I guess they're on th' way," one of the guitar players replies to her before I can answer.

"Cops ain'ta gonna put no stop ta us, neither!" one of the roughs yells from across the street.

"But, brother, we are!" the other guitar player answers back.

"You mangy little honky-tonk, guitar-playin' sot, I'll come over there an' bust that music box over yore bastardly head!"

"I'll furnish th' guitar, mister," the scrawny guitar player replies, "but you'll hafta furnish th' head!"

Laughing, we begin squeezing around the skinny guitar player.

Our collection of sailors, girls, guitar players, and some workmen form three lines in front of The Imperial's door.

Several Japanese men and women stand inside, picking up glass from the floor.

"That's it, folks," the taller guitar player announces. "Squeeze together. Stand right where you are. Don't let that crazy mob get through!"

"Wonder why they threw two cans of corn?" the skinny guitar player asks out loud, not to anybody in particular.

Across the street, one of the roughs mounts the running board of a car before he hollers, "Listen people! I know! Why, just this morning, right here in this neighborhood, a housewife went into a Japanese grocery store. She asked him how much for a can of corn. He told her it was fifteen cents. Then she said that was too much. So he said when his goddam country took th' U.S.A. over, that she would be doing the work in the store, and the corn would cost her thirty-five cents! She hit him over the head with the can of corn! Ha! A good, patriotic, American mother! That's why we smashed that goddam window with th' cans of corn! Nobody can stop us, men! Go on, fight! Get 'em!"

As he's talking, our tall guitar player climbs up on the wheel of a vegetable cart. When the rough is done talking, the tall troubadour calls out, "Listen, folks. These little Japanese farmers that you see up and down the country here and these Japanese people that run the little old cafes and gin joints, they can't help it because they happen to be Japanese. Nine-tenths of them hate their Rising Sun robbers just as much as I do, or you do."

"Lyin' coward! Git down frum dere!" a guy with hairs sticking out from his shirt collar bawls at our guitar guy.

"Pipe down, brother. I'll take care of you later. But this damn story about the can of corn is a rotten, black, and dirty lie! Made up to be used by killers that never hit a day's honest work in their whole lives. I know it's a lie, this can-of-corn story, because even two years ago, I heard the same tale, word for word. Somebody right here in our country is spreading all kinds of just such lies to keep us battling against each other!" the tall guitar guy says.

"Rave on, you silly galoon!"

"You're righter than hell, boy! Pour it on!"

"You're a sneakin' fifth column sonofabitch! Tryin' ta pertect them skunk Japs agint' native-borned American citizens!"

The crowd of roughs starts to move slowly from across the street; we stand ready to keep them back.

The air around us is filled with a heavy sense of an imminent clash of bodies.

Brunette squeezes ever tighter on my waist.

"Stay near me." I tell her, preparing to hide her behind me if anything more should fly.

Just then, an electric train, loaded down with men and railroad tools, pulls past in front of the roughs.

The railroad workers holler a few cracks at the two sides. "What goes on here?" "Gang fight?" "Keep back there, ya'll git run over!"

"Listen ta these ratheads bark!"

The tall guitar player drops down fast off of the hub of the wheel. "Me, I'm going to stand right here," he hollers, "right here on this curb. I just ain't moving."

"I'm with yuh, brother!" One of the older women from the bar walks up behind him carrying a big black purse and a gallon jug of wine.

"I ain't a-movin', neither!" A skinny little old man starts flipping his belt buckle. "Let 'em come!"

The last, two, or three flat cars of men roll down the street and keep the wild mob back for a minute.

The shorter, scrawny, guitar player starts singing:

We will fight together

We shall not be moved

We will fight together

We shall not be moved

Just like a tree

That's planted by the water

We

Shall not

Be moved.

"Everybody sing!" the tall guitar player demands.

We all join in.

As the train with the workers departs, the crowds are just approaching our side of the street.

Singing arm in arm, we stand united, sailors, musicians, drunks, the aged, and even dancing girls, before the door of The Imperial.

We shall not

We shall not be moved
We shall not

We shall not be moved
The union is behind us
We shall not be moved.

The roughs just stand there.

They don't know what to do.

Cussing and threats are thrown our way. "Otta th' way yellow bellied traitors!"

We shall not

We shall not be moved
We shall not

We shall not be moved
We're fighting for our freedom
We shall not be moved.

We continue to sing.

We shall not, we shall not be moved
We shall not, we shall not be moved
We're fighting for our children
We shall not be moved.
We shall not, we shall not be moved
We shall not, we shall not be moved
We'll building a mighty union
We shall not be moved.
We shall not, we shall not be moved
We shall not, we shall not be moved
Black and white together
We shall not be moved.
We shall not, we shall not be moved
We shall not, we shall not be moved
Young and old together
We shall not be moved.

We stay there for over two hours, singing until the crowd of roughs disintegrates into the rainy night.

All of us are drenched, cold, tired, and hungry.

"I need a drink" Sanders calls out.

"I'm buyin'," I project above the rising chatter.

Little brunette pulls my head down toward hers and plants the softest, wettest, and most exhilarating kiss on my lips I ever did feel.

May turn out to be a good night yet!

*****

A Japanese American owned grocery store in Oakland California, December 8, 1941.
https://localwiki.org/oakland/Wanto_Co.

Woody Guthrie and Cisco Houston were scrounging around Los Angeles shortly after the attack on Pearl Harbor, looking for work, and hoping to make a few nickels and dimes singing at saloons along skid row. A gang of people started attacking The Imperial Saloon, a gin joint owned and operated by a Japanese family living right next door. Guthrie, Houston, and the other people at their bar went outside to defend the Japanese family until the police showed up. They defended them by banding together to sing. Few of them probably would have stood strong using non-violence had they not been inspired to do so.

The story and much of the language used in this piece were collected from the book *Bound For Glory* by Woody Guthrie.

Tondelayo

I'm pulled ever higher into the atmosphere by the straining of the Bf-110's two Daimler-Benz 1,085-horsepower engines. To over 26,000 feet, my *Destroyer* climbs to meet the oncoming American B-17 bombers over Kassel.

Let me at 'em!

Snugly resting in my cozy belt inside a drum with 60 other rounds, I'm fourteenth in line to be fired from the nose-mounted left 20-millimeter cannon.

May it be a long burst!

My *Destroyer* zips toward the American bombers; the pilot's firing finger is ready on the flight stick.

Destiny awaits!

Dissipating from the higher pitch of ascent, the engines settle into the lower-octave whirr of level flight.

We must be at altitude. Any time now!

Just a centimeter of distance sits between the pilot's thumb and the firing button on the flight stick.

Less than a centimeter.

The finger touches the button.

Presses down.

Instantly, the cannon's begin their fiery gurgitations. Firing pins strike upon explosive charges, propelling shells at astonishing speeds through the long barrel of the gun, and out the front of the plane with a muzzle flash that would blind anyone staring directly at it.

13, 12, 11, 10, 9, 8, my turn is coming soon!

My belt moves swiftly through the drum, ever closer to the cannon's chamber!

7, 6, 5, 4, 3, 2, 1, MEEEE!!!!!!!!!

Dropped into the chamber, smacked from behind, an explosive charge that I carried with me on my bottom ignites, shooting me at over 600 meters per second out of the barrel.

WWWWWWWHHHHHHHHEEEEEEEEE!!!!!!!!

Instantly frozen by the oxygen-lacking atmosphere of over 26,000 feet, I'm hurtling through the open sky on my way toward one of the American bombers.

I zip past the tail of the plane where a gunner sits on his knees facing out of the back. His guns blaze in a vain attempt to take my ride up here out of the sky. The determined grin on his face belies the inability of his 50-

caliber machine gun to range out far enough to hit my *De-stroyer*.

Within a fraction of a second, I penetrate the metal at the back of the B-17's wing, striking through a bulkhead and then a rubber membrane before lodging myself within the American's fuel tank.

"Hey, Buddy," number 13 says to me when I arrive.

"What are we doing here?" I demand.

"Nothing, that's the problem," 13 replies.

Damn it, I was supposed to explode!

*****

A pair of Bf-110's

A B-17

After a raid on Kassel Germany, a B-17 bomber (*Tondelayo)* returned to its base with eleven unexploded 20-mm shells in its fuel tanks. These may have been from a ground-based or aircraft-based cannon. Any one of these shells should have blown the plane out of the sky. The shells were sent to the armorer to be diffused. When they were opened, each was found to be empty of any explosive charge. Bendiner, Elmer: *The Fall of Fortresses*, Putnam, 1980, pp. 138-139.

The bomber's name, *Tondelayo,* was in honor of a character from the movie <u>*White Cargo*</u>, released in 1942. The beautiful female lead, Tondelayo, was played by Hedy Lemarr.

Slavery

*P*ulling in a breath of floating airborne metal shavings pains my lungs in the same way as taking a deep breath of icy air on a late January morning used to when I played out in the snow as a kid. The straining of my chest from a shock of immense pressure on the inside of my lungs reminds me that I am alive, at least for now.

My shaking hands are not digging in snow, but rather rifling through a box of shell casings. I found that if I let my hand linger in the box for a moment longer than it takes to grasp and remove a casing; I have that extra moment to rest.

All I want to do is sleep.

For more than three years now, it has been the same routine every day, wake up to the sound of a blaring siren while it is still dark. Groggily shuffle my way to the waiting dull-grey truck whose outline is all I can see in the early morning soot that blankets the ground from the nearby steel plant, while staying just beyond the reach of the ever-barking shepherd.

Pile into the truck with the other twenty-four emaciated men of my work brigade, hoping that none of us falls down on the way, to be pounced upon by a trained dog seemingly even hungrier than we are. Spend the day trying to keep my hands steady enough to fill shell casings with explosive charges, but with each passing day finding that my hands want to shake ever more, possibly to cause an explosion, taking me and everyone within a fifty-meter radius around me, out of our misery. After dark, we are herded back into the truck, taken back to our barracks, given a small stale role of sawdust-infused soggy bread, and told to sleep.

My shaking hand is grasped around a shell casing, holding it tightly as I slowly lift the shaped metal cone to my worktable. I can't help but admire the smooth boring lines of the casing, the soft filed-down edges, and the engineering that went into making this 20-millimeter killing container.

Before the German's annexed my country, I was in technical school training to be an engineer. I dreamed of working for Skoda designing and building tanks or airplanes. It was this training that may have saved my life, for whatever that's worth.

Can't I just sleep?

The Germans came to my school and told my class they would house and pay us. They brought us here to Richard, a tunnel complex in the hills near the city of Litomerice in the highlands of the Czech Karst. We believed them.

I just want to shut my eyes.

As my right hand holds the shell casing upright, my left hand reaches down into the small box of waxpaper-wrapped explosive charges. Each charge is already shaped to fit perfectly within the shell casing. It is my job to unwrap each charge before placing it within the shell without touching the edges of the shell's metal to the explosive.

As I reach toward the box, seemingly grasping for the next wrapped charge, I let my left hand slip behind the box so the guard standing to my left as he talks to another guard does not see my hand did not make it into the box. Instead, my hand quickly and quietly shakes its way into my pants, where I have placed a piece of wax paper I was able to smuggle out of the factory last week.

On this paper, I scribbled a message to the universe as much as to myself. It is a reminder; although I am a slave, I have power. This message is what made me open my eyes this morning.

My left hand slips out of my pants holding the wax-paper message, returned to the shape of all of the individual wax-paper charges in the box of explosives. I gently - without shaking - place this paper into the beautifully refined shaped shell casing before putting the casing into the neatly aligned row of casings I have already worked this morning.

My right hand reaches down to the box with the metal casings and pauses there for a moment.
A moment in which, I shut my eyes.

Sleep

My shaking hand lifts the next casing out of the box.

*****

Skoda Works, Plzen, Czechoslovakia
http://forum.nationstates.net/viewtopic.php?f=6&t=255166

After a raid on Kassel Germany, a B-17 bomber *(Tondelayo)* returned to its base with eleven unexploded 20-mm shells in its fuel tanks. These may have been from a ground-based or aircraft-based cannon. Any one of these shells should have blown the plane out of the sky.

The shells were sent to the armorer to be diffused. When they were opened, each was found to be empty of any explosive charge. One of the shells, though, did contain something: a rolled-up slip of paper on which was written, in Czech: "This is all we can do for you now."

Bendiner, Elmer: *The Fall of Fortresses*, Putnam, 1980, pp. 138-139.

Nishi

"*I*t's 11 already!" Susanne, the hurried nurse in white uniform complete with the folded red-crossed nurse's cap, blurts out to me as she rushes up to Mr. Barrymore's room.

"Yep, and he's not in the best mood today." I call back, doubting that the Master of the house can hear me through the thick plaster walls of his Mediterranean-style Beverly Hills villa.

"Take me outside now!" I hear in a yell muffled through the walls.

I better hurry on his lemonade, or I won't hear the end of it until his nap at 2.

Quickly, I begin picking out the ripest lemons from the box delivered this morning.

Mr. Barrymore's mood seems to shift rapidly from a confused and docile old man enjoying the last wisps of life to a frustrated curmudgeon energetically angry at a world he no longer understands.

My fingers burn from the acidic lemon juice pouring over them into the measuring cup as I slowly turn the juicer with my left hand and the lemon with my right.

"Mary, can you help with the stairs?" Susanne calls to me from atop the staircase.

"I'll be right there."

Choosing between finishing his lemonade and allowing him his daily time outside is never easy. Why don't I ever start making the lemonade earlier?

Shuffling to the bottom of the staircase, I wipe my lemon-scented hands on a dishtowel, which I then stuff into the beige apron wrapped around my waist.

The Master's wheelchair is descending slowly down the side of the staircase with machine precision so his frail body is not jostled as he moves from one level of the house to the next.

This German-built contraption may be the last piece of German machinery imported to the

United States before the Germans declared war on us.

Having just been installed, the wheelchair elevator is a machine Mr. Barrymore accepts, but he does not appreciate having to use.

"This damn NAZI machine is not needed in my home. I can take these stairs myself!" he barks out.

"Yes Sir," Susanne replies. "We'll walk back up on our return."

Missing the irony in this response, Mr. Barrymore grunts an affirmation, before looking up at me.

"Where is my lemonade?" he demands.

"I'll have it ready as we step outside" I reply as I take his right hand to help him dismount from the wheelchair connected to the wall.

Susanne rushes down the staircase taking his left arm in her own to guide him out the door.

Scurrying back to the kitchen to put the final touches on the lemonade, I can hear the front door open as the two of them burst into the garden.

I pour in three soup-spoonfuls of white Hawaiian sugar, mix in a cup of ice-cold water with the lemon juice, and stir the mixture into a tall pitcher before pouring the sugary concoction into a carafe I place on a tray next to a spotless drinking glass.

The Master cannot accept spots on his drinking glasses; a lesson I learned only too well again yesterday when I had to clean up the shattered remnants of one off the walkway outside the front door.

Carrying the tray out the front door, I overhear Mr. Barrymore ask, "What are those soldiers doing with Nishi and his family?"

I had completely forgotten today is the day that Nishi, the gardener, and his family are being taken away.

"They're going away," Susanne replies.

"Why?" Mr. Barrymore asks, a look of concern on his face.

Mr. Barrymore looks across the well-trimmed hedges toward the driveway, where a large ugly green truck sits surrounded by soldiers. Nishi, his wife, and two sons fervently gather their meager belongings at the behest of multiple gun-toting boys in uniforms matching the wretched truck.

Susanne looks up at me, hoping I can save her from having to explain to Mr. Barrymore why he is losing his gardener.

"Sir, Nishi is Japanese. We are at war with Japan." I softly offer as I set the tray of lemonade on a side table. At the same time, Susanne lowers Mr. Barrymore into a chair on the freshly mown lawn.

"But is there a war on with Nishi and his family?" Mr. Barrymore asks.

Susanne and I look at each other.

How do I answer that?

*****

Bella Vista
https://www.pinterest.com/pin/467741111281721192/

One day in the early spring of 1942, at the door of John Barrymore's California mansion, Barrymore saw his Japanese-American gardener Nishi with his family and their belongings waiting to be carried away by soldiers. Barrymore was dying, his mind fading in and out of reality, and he did not understand what was happening. When someone explained America was at war with Japan, Barrymore could only murmur, "But is there a war on with Nishi and his family?"

On February 19, 1942, President Roosevelt signed Executive Order 9066, authorizing the Secretary of War to prescribe certain *military areas* and to exile *any or all* persons from them. Though couched in broad language, the order was aimed at Japanese-Americans. Under this order, in the spring and summer of 1942, 112,000 Japanese-Americans were removed to internment camps throughout the country, eventually ending up in 10 permanent camps away from the coasts. Germans, Italians, Romanians, Bulgarians, and Hungarians were all exempt from this roundup.

Not a single Japanese-American was ever brought to trial on charges of espionage or sabotage in the United States. Thousands of Japanese Americans fought and died for the United States in World War II while their family members were held in camps for the duration of the war. One of whom, Daniel Inouye, was awarded the Medal of Honor and became the highest-ranking Asian-American in United States politics.

Tank vs. Battleship

*W*hen I first saw the small object noisily lumbering up the road toward Milhaud pier, I laughed inside.

How could the Germans expect to take me with that little thing?

My skeleton crew is working feverishly to plant explosives throughout my body. Grenades are being placed at strategic points in my machinery. Fused charges are being lowered into my turret magazines. My sea cocks are also being opened to the water of Toulon harbor.

That puny steel vehicle rushing at me with all the speed and grandeur it can muster is comical in comparison.

From the human scale, that little Tiger tank with its 88mm gun must command respect. From the scale of my majestic size and ample allowance of 330mm guns, I am just not impressed.

The hatch on the top of the tank opens as the gnat pulls up on my port side along the pier.

"Surrender the ship," the commander of the tank calls out in German.

Admiral Jean de Laborde, Commander in Chief of the High Seas Fleet, ordered all of the fleet's captains to "SCUTTLE! SCUTTLE! SCUTTLE!" early this morning when intelligence came that German armored units were heading toward the harbor. The Germans entered the *Free Zone* of Vichy France, today in response to the Allied invasion of North Africa.

November 27, 1942, marks the end of any illusion France is free.

Admiral de Laborde replies, "You will not take this ship."

The tank's commander orders his crew to fire their puny gun.

Machine gunners atop my multiple decks open up on the armored pest sitting along my side.

I could kill that pesky gnat, if only I could lower my anti-aircraft guns.

Urgh, one shot from my main guns would swipe him, and half the block he's on, away from the world for good. .

The Tiger's 88mm gun rips a hole in turret 2, wounding six sailors and killing Lieutenant Frinage, who had been in charge of demolition of that turret. The Germans helped the Lieutenant complete his task when they killed him. That turret is no longer useful.

That gnat has a nasty bite.

I could tear you to shreds you little fleck!

At this senseless loss of life, Admiral de La-borde orders the machine gunners to stop firing.

We're not going to fight this little piss-ant?

Explosions begin convulsing my hull. Turrets 1, 3, and 4 explode in a swarm of jagged steel as the magazines in each are strewn asunder with their own stored gunpowder.

My machine room and engines are blown away with well-placed grenades, rendering me dead in the water.

My sea cocks are released, allowing water to flow into my lower decks. My keel settles all of my 26,500 tons upon the floor of Toulon harbor. I am to sail no more.

That pesky little tank still sits there, gun aimed at me, its commander screaming at his crew because they failed to capture me intact.

I wish I could have just swiped you away, you Nazi toy.

My guns are no longer operable. I can no longer sail. I cannot even propel myself or leave the floor of the harbor.

My only reprieve is that it is my crew that ended my career rather than surrendering what was once an awesome and awe-inspiring destructive capability to our country's occupiers.

At least, the bottom of this harbor is soft. I may have to rest here for a while.

A German Panzer IV tank faces the sunken hulk of a French cruiser, sitting at the bottom of Toulon Harbor.
http://modelsuwemilitaria.blogspot.ie/2013_10_01_archive.html?view=classic

On November 27, 1942, the Germans responded to the Allied invasion of North Africa by occupying what was left of Vichy France. Of particular interest to the Germans, the French Fleet was ordered scuttled (destroyed by its own men), rather than fall into German and Italian hands. The Germans rushed to the port facilities, hoping to take some of the ships, particularly the *Strasbourg,* intact.

In one of the strangest engagements of the war, a German tank raced to the ship, turned its gun on the battleship, and forced the crew of the mighty war machine to surrender. The French crew, though, destroyed the ship before the Germans could board, rendering the hulk useless to the Axis.

Enemy Honor

*T*he gold braid and stark white of Admiral Morgan's crisp uniform contrasts sharply with the cracked and filthy, formerly white walls of the Taranto naval barracks. In front of these crumbling edifices that now house my team of Frogmen, we stand to await his passing at the side of Crown Prince Umberto. The Crown Prince is here to give my team medals for heroism and valor. The Admiral and I met four years ago under very different circumstances. He was Captain of the *HMS Valiant* when my team of Sea Devils was sent to sink his ship.

> *"Hello! Jack Tar, what a beautiful day!*
>
> *We frogmen are coming to teach you to swim,*
>
> *So we hope you're all right, and we hope that you're trim*
>
> *We dive, but you go down to stay."*

The creed of the 10th Light Flotilla rings through the thin metal walls of *Scirè*, the submarine carrying our Pigs and my devilish team. At twenty-two feet long and twenty-one inches in diameter, each dark-painted Pig is propelled by silent electric motors enabling it to slide quietly through the water at a rate slower than the average swimmer. With a range of ten miles, we are not expecting to bring any Pigs back with us from this mission. Detachable warheads carry 660 pounds of explosives, just enough to blow a massive hole in any warship unlucky enough to be targeted by my motley crew.

We joined the *Scirè* on December 14 on the Greek island of Leros where it had been undergoing minor repairs. After removing and then repacking our Pigs in giant tubes mounted to the deck of the submarine (*I don't trust anyone else to pack my gear*), we carried our rubber suits and breathing apparatus with us into the cramped and overcrowded submarine. There are no permanent quarters on the ship, so we sleep in shifts, along with the rest of the crew, in hammocks strung up in the aft torpedo room.

The *Scirè* requires more repairs than originally planned, so we have to wait an extra 24 hours before we can set off on our mission. This delay gives my team time to review our mission and check all our gear. We repack the Pigs one more time to ensure they are exactly how we want them when we are removing them under water within sight of our target, and the enemy.

The delay also provides time for me to write my mother three letters.

My Dear Mother: By the time you receive this letter, I will be dead. I volunteered for a dangerous mission, which failed...

My Dear Mother: By the time you receive this letter, I will be back at my base. I volunteered for a dangerous mission, which was a success...

My Dear Mother: By the time you receive this letter, I will be a prisoner of war...

I give all three letters to the naval post officer, ordering him to mail only the appropriate one when the results of my mission are known.

At dawn on the 16th, we are finally able to slip away from Leros toward the Egyptian coast. My anxiety rises in transit when we receive notice of un-favorable sea conditions. Another 24-hour delay is imposed on us, grinding my nerves with the notion I will have to wait one more day to find out if I am to die. The odds are slim any of us will return, let alone be alive in a few days.

Before we left Taranto for Leros, we were ordered to make wills and pack our belongings for shipment home in case we do not return. I had a difficult time deciding where to ship my things. As a naval officer, I am not supposed to be married, but I cannot fathom the idea of dying without leaving a son behind. My sweet Valeria will only expose our secret marriage to collect the insurance money if I don't make it back. I could not, though, send her my belongings. She will have enough on her hands in a few months. Therefore, along with the letters, I addressed the shipment to my mother.

After sailing to the Egyptian coast, the *Scirè* advances slowly toward the port of Alexandria. When it is just outside of 12 miles, the Captain of the *Scirè*, Junio Valerio Borghese, decides to take the submarine under the surface and run it silent. His sincere fear of being spotted or encountering minefields does not deter us from achieving our proper positioning right outside the harbor gate after 23 hours of silent navigation.

We arrive just a mile outside of the harbor of Alexandria on the 18th. My 10th Light Flotilla team is only thinking of the mission. We have prepared for this attack for over six years. Our training and previous success at Suda Bay bring us the courage to engage in this moment. The latest naval intelligence reports from our Command in Athens confirm the presence of the battleships *HMS Valiant* and *HMS Queen Elizabeth* in the harbor. These are what remain of the main elements of British naval power in the Mediterranean since our German submarine friends sank the aircraft carrier *HMS Ark Royal* and the battleship *HMS Barham* in November. If these two remaining battleships could be taken out, the Italian and German convoys supplying Rommel's forces in Libya could sail safely. We could capture Cairo, drive the

British out of North Africa, and cut the British Empire in two by taking the Suez Canal. The British know and fear such an outcome. Therefore, they placed their remaining battleships in what they believe to be the safety of the well-guarded harbor of Alexandria. My devilish band is here to belie that belief.

At twenty-seven, I am the old man of the team, but not the only officer to have come out of the Academy at Livorno. Assigned to attack the *Valiant* with me is Petty Officer Emilo Bianchi. Targeting the *Queen Elizabeth,* Lieutenants Antonio Marceglia and Spartaco Schergat are donning their rubber suits on my left. Lieutenants Vincenzo Martellotta and Mario Marino, who are to direct their attack at the 16,000-ton fleet tanker *Sagona,* are directly behind me. We are teams 1, 2, and 3 respectively.

We have planned the attack well. Each team knows the primary mission by heart. Once in position under the enemy ship, we are to gingerly detach the 660-pound explosive from the Pig's nose, secure it to the ship's keel, and set the timer. Then, still mounted on the Pig, we are to start the motor, glide away from the ship, and surface.

The time fuses are already set. The *Sagona* will explode at about 5.55 a.m., the *Valiant* at 6.05, the *Elizabeth* at 6.15. We are also carrying floating incendiary bombs to scatter in the tanker's spilled oil to ignite a fire across the whole harbor. What we have not practiced well is what occurs after our attack. There are vague plans to steal a fishing boat and rendezvous with the *Scirè* on the 24th, but those details have yet to be worked out. After all, it is only after achieving our primary and secondary missions that we can really begin to think about escape. *We know full well that none of us will probably make it that far.*

I slide my six-foot frame into the rubber suit, an action my muscles are so used to I no longer catch my left foot on the odd angle of the knee as I slip my leg into the dark inflexible material. Pulling up the suit so my body is covered is a two-person job. The rubber resists every attempt to change its shape. Emilo helps me place my breathing device and my watch, which is synchronized with the team and the submarine. It is now 9:21 p.m., and we are set to exit the *Scirè*.

The air hatch is unsealed so each man can exit the submarine in turn. The *Scirè* is sitting just above the floor of the ocean, one mile from Alexandria harbor. As each of us escapes the confines of the metal tube for the compressing pressure of the ocean, we feel relieved we are finally starting what we have been trained to do.

As we unpack the Pigs from the tubes on the deck of the submarine, the hatch on Pig 3 fails to open. Marino is not one to accept failure, particularly before the mission even starts, so he attempts to pry the hatch open with his knife. The knife slips, slashing across his arm. The rubber suit is compromised, his arm is cut, and he looks to be in quite a bit of pain.

Because we cannot talk to each other under water, I tap Marino on the shoulder and point to the submarine's air hatch. I am offering him a chance to go back into the *Scirè* to get patched up and sit this mission out. He waves me off and starts again on the stuck hatch.

Martellotta brings over a bandage, and they fix Marino up.

We are able to open the hatch on Pig 3 by prying it open with the handle of a wrench.

I look at Marino's arm and his suit. He gives me a thumbs up.

I wave to each man before signaling to move out.

My head protrudes above the water as I sit astride the Pig. Our little craft move slowly toward the harbor lighthouse as we sing to ourselves.

"Hello! Jack Tar, what a beautiful day!

We frogmen are coming to teach you to swim,

So we hope you're all right and we hope that you're trim

We dive, but you go down to stay."

We make slow progress toward the harbor. When we are about a quarter of a mile from the steel net protecting the harbor entrance, I order the teams to stop. This is the best chance we have of eating before we are too busy to think about food. It is now almost midnight, and the growl of my stomach would betray me to any guards with a keen sense of hearing.

As a group, floating on our bomb-laden Pigs we have brought to a line side by side, we eat what could be our last meal. I pry open a sealed canister of cold chicken. Emilo shares the bread he is carrying. Antonio produces small bottles of champagne given to him by Captain Borghese.

Food, even canned food, brings forth an extreme pleasure when consumed atop a bomb-laden torpedo bobbing in the ocean outside of a well-guarded harbor housing ones target of destruction and potential resting place. I don't believe I've ever tasted a more satisfying meal.

We finish our food, packing the debris into a sack we weigh down with an incendiary bomb before letting it fall to the bottom of the ocean floor.

The moment has arrived to approach the steel net and make our way into the harbor. Each of the Pigs carries pneumatic cutting shears we could use to make a hole in the net, but they are so noisy I would prefer not to use them if I can avoid it. I quieted my stomach so there is no sense in giving myself away with a pneumatic device in the still of the night. Not to mention, in our failed attack on Gibraltar, we learned the hard way the British plant explosives on their net to kill anyone attempting to sabotage it.

I waive my hand to order a halt. The teams stop.

I need to decide exactly how to tackle the net.

A moment goes by, then two.

As I am questioning using the pneumatic cutters, the lighthouse and the harbor suddenly light up before us. The whole area is awash in light.

They could not have seen my team yet!

The anti-submarine net begins moving.

They're opening the net!

Three British destroyers appear out of the darkness, heading for the harbor entrance.

I wave my team forward. We slip through the ever-widening opening in the net.

I cannot believe they opened the net for us.

The frothy wakes of three destroyers toss our little Pigs as we use them for cover for our entrance into the harbor. Our enthusiasm for such luck is tempered by the wild ride we endure following so close to the ships. Every moment, I look up at the ships, half-expecting to see a searchlight illuminate my team, exposing us to deadly attack in this open and highly vulnerable position.

Only my eyes and ears are above the water. Yet, even at night, under blackout conditions, it is still easy to single out a ship for destruction. There may be the gleam of a match to be seen or a line of singing heard. These marks remind me what I seek to destroy is alive.

Pulling out of the wake of the destroyer, I am able to calm the motion of our Pig. Using this moment of relative peace, I take a compass bearing. I should be only a short distance from the *Valiant*. Turning to my left, I can make out the grey outline of her majestic scale in the dark haze of the night. I begin maneuvering my little Pig toward the great ship and its ultimate demise.

About 300 meters away from the ship, Emilo and I run into a protective net. This is not worth cutting with a pneumatic device at all. We are so close to the ship everyone on board would hear us.

I turn around to Emilo and raise my hand. To myself I say, "Let's lift the net."

Emilo and I strain, but the net will not budge. The mesh wire leaves a lead feeling in my hand for about thirty seconds after we let go.

We cannot be foiled so close to our target.

Emilo raises his hand before letting it fall again.

"Good idea!" I reply, knowing full well my words never made it to his ears.

We pull the Pig up so it is horizontal to the net. Then, putting our arms under it, we lift it out of the water, gingerly rolling it over the net, so it does not splash on the way down. The whole time my heart and mind are racing. *Don't make a sound! Don't make a sound! Don't make a sound!*

No sound is made. We did it. We are inside the torpedo net!

I get back on top of the Pig and immediately flood the diving tank. The water closes over my head.

Everything is cold, dark, and silent.

While we were training for this mission, we researched the design specifications of the *Valiant*. We concluded the best place to attach the warhead is below the Number 1 turret. Unfortunately, I did not look at where we were in relation to that turret before diving under the water.

I need to see where the turret is.

Emilo stays with the Pig as I surface to see where we are in relation to the mountain of a ship towering above us.

In order not to lose contact with the Pig, I unreal a coil of cord I can follow back when I am done.

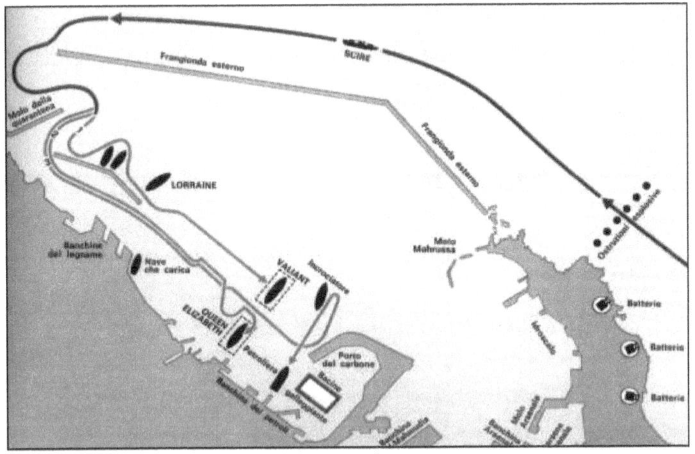

Alexandria Harbor map
http://www.xray-mag.com/content/first-frogmen-part-2

I surface just enough for my eyes to make out the massive outline of the *Valiant*. We are about 30 meters out of position, so we will have to adjust. Returning to the Pig, I assume my position behind the steering console where I turn the grip to propel the sloth-like beast forward.

119

Nothing happens.

I turn the grip again.

Again, nothing happens.

The cord must have gotten caught in the propeller.

Turning to point Emilo toward the propeller, I am shocked to find that he is not there.

"Shit!" I blurt out to no one in particular.

Where in the hell could he have gone?

I have to do this myself now.

Damn it!

I reach for the propeller, but I cannot budge the cord.

Instead of messing with the propulsion system to move the last 30 meters, I decide to just remove the warhead and take it to the ship myself.

Removing my insulated rubber gloves to allow myself to manipulate the warhead, I am reminded of why we wear rubber suits. The water is freezing. My hands begin to go numb quickly.

Initially, I am able to move the 660-pound warhead just a few centimeters through the mud floor of the harbor. I keep pushing. I take a break to put my hands in the gloves again. I push more to achieve a couple more centimeters. I take another break.

After several rounds of pushing and resting to warm my hands, I develop a rhythm of a few centimeters, a short break, a few centimeters, and another short break. It takes me almost an hour to move the warhead alone. I am exhausted, my muscles are screaming, and my hands have no feeling left in them.

By the time the warhead is below turret 1 of the *Valiant,* I lack the strength to lift it in order to attach it to the hull. Our mission calls for the warhead to be attached to the ship. It also calls for two men to be here to lift it into place. Because the floor of the harbor is only about five feet below the keel of the ship, I think the 660 pounds of explosives will still do severe damage.

Maybe I am rationalizing. Maybe I am right. Either way, I can't lift it.

It is now 3 a.m., which means that there is still about three hours to go until this bomb goes off.

I have to get out of here!

Close to collapsing from exhaustion, I use the last of my energy to surface. I don't put any energy toward silence, for I have none left to spare. A small splash occurs as my head breaks the water.

I just don't care anymore, I am so tired.

A searchlight from the *Valiant* flares to life before I have a chance to move. The brilliant white beam sheds its ominous light directly at me.

Shit, Shit!

A hail of bullets comes whizzing toward me.

Shit, Shit!

I gather what remaining energy adrenaline has produced in my body to flail out toward an anchor buoy I see out of the corner of my eye. It is not much, but it can provide some small amount of protection. As I approach the buoy, I see Emilo with his mask off, holding on the other side of it.

I rip my mask off so I can yell out "What the hell are you doing here?"

"My air tank broke. I fainted. When I woke up, I was bobbing on the surface. I swam here to hide," he replies.

"Well, thanks a lot for all of your help down there!"

"I would not have been any help. My left arm is broken." Emilo retorts.

A small boat enters the water from the *Valiant's* side. It takes only a few brief moments for its crew of five to find our position.

They throw a line to Emilo first. With his broken left arm dangling at his side, he uses his right arm, mouth, and feet to claw his way aboard. Then they throw the line to me. The strength in my arms is so sapped all I can do is hold on to the line. I let the boat's crew pull me aboard. We are brought alongside the battleship and told to climb aboard. Emilo climbs the ladder using his right arm and both legs. Assessing what energy I have left, I look up at the length of the ladder. I know if I refuse they will probably just shoot me. I don't know where I obtain the strength, but somehow, I am able to climb the ladder, slowly rising up to the quarterdeck of the *Valiant*, where I collapse.

I cannot go any further.

I am now on the very ship that I set to explode in less than three hours.

An officer approaches us. Emilo is sitting. I am sprawled out, lying on the deck. The officer orders us to stand up. Emilo and I stumble to our feet.

What a dejected lot we look to be.

"Who are you, and what are you doing here?" the officer barks.

We provide our ranks and serial numbers, but nothing more.

Without wasting time to ask more questions, the officer orders us away. Emilo is taken somewhere away from me. I am walked to a storeroom on what appears to be a deck below the water line of the ship. An orderly comes in with a glass of rum and a packet of cigarettes. I down the drink in one gulp, shivering from the slight shock to my system. Lighting one of the cigarettes, I sit down in the only chair in the otherwise crowded room of junk. The orderly leaves me there, I guess to think about what I have done.

My watch now says 5:30; there is a little over a half hour until the bomb goes off. I sit, nervously, my eyes glued to my watch. The cigarettes burn so fast I am through a quarter of the pack by 5:40. At 5:43, Emilo, flanked by a guard, joins me in the storeroom.

"They took me to the sick bay and questioned me more," he says.

"How are you feeling?" I reply.

"Rum helps," is his rejoinder.

Another chair is brought in for Emilo. I hand him a cigarette as we stare at each other and our watches.

After a minute, I offer, "There was no hope for us, but we can soon die happy knowing that our mission will be accomplished."

Emilo grins, but says nothing.

At 5:54 am, a loud rumble can be heard in the distance.

Martellotta's team must have been successful against the tanker ship.

"I have to warn the captain." I exclaim as I maneuver toward the door. Emilo nods in agreement.

Pounding on the door, I demand to see the captain.

To my surprise, the guard outside of the door quickly takes me to the captain's office. I see that his name is Morgan.

"So you want to tal. . . " Is the greeting I receive from the captain, but I don't wait for him to finish.

Interrupting him, I bellow, "Your ship will blow up in less than ten minutes. I have no desire to kill men unnecessarily. I suggest you get all hands on deck."

"Where is the charge placed?" Morgan asks patiently.

I pause.

"If you refuse to answer, I will send you back below"

If he knows the charge is lying on the bottom of the harbor below the ship, he can move the ship.

"Get him back below then" the captain orders.

As the guard is taking me back down to the storeroom, I hear an announcement on the ship's loudspeaker.

"All hands to the upper decks. All hands to leave the lower decks immediately."

The guard violently throws me into the storage room, slams the door, and then runs off.

I look at Emilo. He looks at me. We both light a new cigarette. There are only three left in the pack now.

My watch says that it is 6:04 a.m. I feel my life literally ticking away with each second passing on the watch.

6:04 and 32 seconds, 33, 34, 35. . . 57, 58, 59

6:05

Nothing.

Emilo eyes me.

I look back.

Did I set the fuse properly? Of course, I did. How could I not? I could not set it to the exact second, but it has to be . . .

6:06

A violent explosion convulses the entire battleship. I am launched out of my chair and thrown against the wall of the storeroom. Darkness envelops me. I stir, but nothing moves. My eyes open to acrid dark smoke filling the room. Emilo is impossible to see, but I can make out the lines where the door was closed. Light is entering the room through there. The blast must have opened the door.

Remembering the route the guard had taken me to the storeroom from the deck, I retrace those same steps. I am surprised that I am not stopped along the way. In fact, as I go by, British personnel stand up to make way for me.

They must know I saved their lives.

When I make it on deck, there is so much confusion and disorder I can stand there looking out over the beginning of daybreak at the sulfuric smoke emanating from the tanker and from the *Valiant*. The hustle of crew running in every direction fades to the background while I take in a deep breath and lean against a bulkhead.

From where I am standing, only feet away from the stairwell I used to come on deck, I can see the stern of the ship and the third target for my Sea Devils, the battleship *Queen Elizabeth*. Right at 6:15, a terrific explosion rocks that ship too.

Marceglia has done it! All three teams were successful!

I must have missed the *Valiant* settle after the explosion as I was making my way above deck, but watching the *Queen Elizabeth*, I realize that the shallow harbor is a blessing for the British. All three ships my Devils attacked simply seem to have descended 4-5 feet to sit upright on the muddy harbor floor.

My Sea Devils did it. At this moment, the Regia Marina is the dominant force in the Mediterranean. We sank their two battleships!

I am still alive!

I belt out:

"Hello! Jack Tar, what a beautiful day!

My whole team survived the attacks against Alexandria harbor. We were all captured and found out that despite our complete success, we took no lives. We sank every ship assigned to us, but killed no one in the process. We were interred for the remainder of Italy's alliance with Germany. Winston Churchill even commented on my team, calling us "An extraordinary example of courage and ingenuity."

I was initially sent to Cairo and then to Palestine before escaping to Syria. In Syria, I was caught and put aboard a ship heading to India, where I again escaped. During my time in custody as a prisoner of war, I would occasionally receive a letter from Valeria. Every now and then, she would mention the clever things *Renzo* had done. Renzo is my little brother's name, but I did not realize at the time, it is also the name of my year-old son.

When Italy declared war on Germany in October 1943, becoming a co-belligerent with Britain, I volunteered to help the British Royal Navy with its underwater weapons program and volunteered to help plan and carry out an important mission to thwart German plans to block the harbor of La Spezia. As a mixed team of Italian and British frogmen, we slipped in and sank the cruisers *Gorizia* and *Bolzano* before they could be maneuvered into the harbor entrance and scuttled. Our raid secured the utility of La Spezia as an allied port to supply future offensives against the turncoat Germans in Italy.

Gold braid on Admiral Morgan's crisp uniform contrasts sharply with the cracked and filthy formerly white walls of the Taranto naval barracks. In front of these crumbling edifices that now contain my existence, my team of frogmen stands to await his passing at the side of Crown Prince Umberto. The Crown Prince is here to give my team medals for heroism and valor. The Admiral and I met four years ago under very different circumstances. He was Captain of the *HMS Valiant* when my team of Sea Devils was sent to sink his ship.

It turns out Admiral Morgan never forgot how I gave him time to evacuate the *Valiant's* lower decks, thereby saving the lives of his 1,700-man crew. He had tried to give me a British medal for my role in the La Spezia raid, but was stopped from doing so because Italy was merely a co-belligerent against Germany, rather than an Ally and member of The United Nations.

Today, Admiral Morgan stands at the side of Crown Prince Umberto, who knows of the Admiral's appreciation for what I had done.

As I step forward to receive the *Valor Militare*, Italy's highest decoration, for leading the raid on Alexandria, the Crown Prince turns to the admiral and exclaims, "Come on Morgan, this is your show."

The Admiral steps forward, takes the medal from the Crown Prince, and places it upon my chest. I was thus decorated by Admiral Morgan for what he

called *a very courageous and gallant attack* on his
ship.

*****

Luigi Durand de la Penne
https://husarblog.files.wordpress.com/2011/09/de-la-penne.jpg

In the aftermath of the attack on Alexandria Harbor, the Italian Navy could have been unchallenged in the Mediterranean. With the protection its cruisers could offer, there was nothing standing in the way of Italian dominance of the Sea. Italy could have sent almost unmolested convoys to Axis troops fighting in North Africa, supplying them with everything they could need for victory, but those cruisers never sallied forth. Air reconnaissance pictures taken the very next day were correctly interpreted by Italian intelligence officers to show that both the *Valiant* and the *Queen Elizabeth* had been heavily damaged and would be out of action for several months at least. Mussolini demanded to see the pictures himself, and as an untrained aerial photoreconnaissance neophyte, he only saw that the ships were upright. He overruled his experts. The ships, he decreed, were unharmed. Because his word could not be challenged, the Italian fleet remained in port. They missed their golden opportunity to help the Axis seize the Suez Canal and cut off the British from its empire and oil supply.

The British did everything possible to encourage Mussolini's belief that he was smarter than his experts. While high-paced underwater work was done to repair the holes ripped in the bottoms of the two battleships, above the water everything was made to look like normal routine. Both ships kept up steam.

Band concerts and receptions were held on their decks. Full ceremonial colors, sunset bugle calls, and parades took place on the upper decks. Even gun drills were carried out. More than a year went by before either ship was again ready for action, a year in which the Axis lost the battle for North Africa.

Over the Top

*A*s I work my way up the stairs from the crew quarters to the chart room, a soft rumble fills my ears. It is not the normal clank-clank-clank of the diesel engines churning two decks below of which I am just becoming accustomed, but a very low bass of ever-increasing intensity that sounds like nothing I have heard before.

"Kid, get to those charts and let me know exactly where we are," orders the Captain.

Captain, he's but five years older than me, and I'm only 18. He puts on this air of respectability and confidence even though he's still figuring out how to steer this behemoth through the narrow channels between the Great Lakes toward the Brooklyn Navy Yard.

"Yes Sir," I reply briskly, hoping to sound enthusiastic, even if I'm not.

I never wanted to be a navigator. I joined the Navy to fly, but was rejected for flight training. Instead, they stuck me on this LST making its way from Chicago to New York via the Great Lakes and Erie Canal. This is my contribution to the War. What a joke!

Looking down at the navigation chart, I'm lost among all the little signs and symbols.

I did not pay much attention in navigation training. I asked four times to get transferred to gunnery, flight, logistics, and even subs, but was rejected each time. Eventually, they passed me out of navigation in three times the length it takes the average navigator to graduate. I guess they figured it was easier to get rid of me than have me pestering them about going somewhere else to do almost anything else.

"Well, where are we?" the Captain demands.

"Sir, we are approximately two miles south of the canal entrance." I reply, pulling that number out of thin air.

"Good, I can't make out a damn thing in this fog."

Neither can I, so how do you think I can possibly tell you where we are, you pretentious prick?

Pausing for a moment, I can hear the clanking of the engines as well as the ever increasing deep bass of incessant rumbling I cannot figure out.

My hand slides slowly across the chart, stopping where the last shift left off on their markings with the grease pencil. As I hold this point with my right forefinger, I look across the chart room toward the gauge with the ship's speed.

I might as well try to figure out where we are, considering we have to turn for the Erie Canal at some point, and this fog is going to make that almost impossible to see.

Ok, so if we're going at eight 8 knots, and they last noted our location about a half hour ago, we must have gone four miles. Right?

Using my thumb and forefinger, rather than the protractor I left in my locker, I estimate the turn off for the Erie Canal to be approximately six miles away from the last marked position on the chart.

Wow, I'm better at this navigating thing than I thought. I was right with that guess!

The incessant bass rumbling is getting louder now, almost causing me to miss the Captain when he calls out.

"Are you sure we're still coming up to the turn off, and haven't passed it?"

"Yes Sir, we still have not seen Buffalo yet, so we're not even up the channel to the turn," I reply.

This fog is so thick I wonder if we will see Buffalo. How am I going to know when to turn into the channel if I can't see the city or the channel lights?

My eyes leave the Captain and return to the chart.

If we missed the turn, we'd be going around Grand Island, and I did not feel the ship make a left. I mean port; I must remember that.

The rumbling is getting even louder, almost deafening.

"I don't like this, Navigator," the Captain yells. "Let me see those charts!" I move aside just in time to miss getting hit by the Captain's charging frame. He's got the body of a linebacker and doesn't seem to be afraid to use it.

He looks down at the chart, noting where the last position was marked. He looks at the clock, at the speed gauge, and then at me.

"Flank Reverse! Flank Reverse!" he yells at the top of his lungs.

"Aye Sir, Flank Reverse." the con replies.

My guts fall out of me as the ship lurches backwards. Instruments are falling off the walls, and crewmembers are tripping over themselves. I hold the chart table with both hands so as not to fall to the deck.

"You multiplied wrong!" the Captain yells, staring directly at me.

I don't know what to say. I really thought I got it right this time. We were two miles away from the turn off.

Seeing I have no explanation for myself, the Captain turns from me.

"Get this incompetent fool off my bridge!" the Captain barks to no one in particular.

I didn't multiply wrong, did I? I mean I halved the speed and then figured the . . . Oh, damn it. A knot is 1.15077945 miles per hour, not 1 mile per hour. Stupid British and their navigation rules!

The ship's speed slows, but we are not stopping, even at flank reverse.

The current in the channel is moving faster than the ship can propel itself backwards.

So, if I added wrong, then what is our current position?

Without looking at the chart, I do the math in my head. We're over 2 miles past the turn off for the

Erie Canal, which means, we're almost right on Niagara Falls.

A deafening roar fills the chart room as mist begins seeping in through the closed windows.

Almost, shit, we're at the falls!

"A…nds…ace……pact…… is no….ill!" the Captain calls on the loud speakers.

With fog surrounding the ship, I can't make out how close or far we are from the falls. I can't see anything. I can't hear anything over the deep roar.

The front of the ship disappears into a white sheet of infinity.

Slowly, the white swallows more of the ship.

I turn to the Captain, who is yelling something into the loud speakers.

As the middle of the ship disappears into the white void, I feel the deck of the ship rise up, pushing me into the sky.

The whole stern of the ship is rising, faster, faster, faster, now.

I'm holding on with all my might to the chart table as its angle goes from perpendicular to me to 45 degrees, and then parallel.

For a moment, the whole world is suspended in mid-air. Nothing moves. Not a sound can be heard.

I'm holding on for my life, and all is serene. I am suspended in time and space.

Then, the navigation chart begins to slide, slowly at first. It picks up speed as it brushes away from the table until it hits the floor.

Instantly, the whole room drops.

My arms go from hanging on from below the table to sliding right off of its top as I fall up toward the bulkhead of the ship.

Crashing into the dull grey painted metal of the bulkhead, my shoulder snaps. My eyes open as I lie on the floor of the crew cabin, at the foot of my bunk.

"Tanner fell out of bed!" someone yells from across the room.

A room full of enlisted men howls with laughter as I look around to get my bearings.

I slowly stand up and look at the clock on the wall.

I have under a half-hour until my shift in the chart room begins. I better get going.

Remember, one knot is not 1 mile per hour!

*****

An LST landing a tank on a beach.
https://commons.wiki-
media.org/wiki/File:LST_Sicily.jpg

With most of America's major shipyards pro-
ducing large fighting ships for the Navy, the produc-
tion of landing craft had to be portioned out to
smaller yards across the country. Contracts for these

ships were given to small boatyards and manufacturing companies on the inland waterways, which had never made anything, like LSTs before.

The ships were built along the Ohio River, for example at Pittsburgh and Ambridge, Pennsylvania, at Jeffersonville and Evansville, Indiana. One of the biggest yards was at *Chicago Bridge and Iron* shipyard in Seneca, Illinois. These ships would be built along a river, slid on ramps into the waterway, and then sailed down to the sea by green crews. One of these inexperienced crews from the Great Lakes missed turning into the Erie Canal in the Niagara River at night and would have gone over the falls if it hadn't run aground instead.

The Offer

"*A*h, so that is what brought you to Washington, Mr. President?" The balding, crisply uniformed Lieutenant General laughs out loud following a simple joke that caps a lovely dinner in the sunroom of his white colonial home in Falls Church, Virginia. A humid, Washington June evening with the sun's rays still shining through the glass-enclosed side of the home offers natural light in a slowly descending summer night.

This is about as far as I can get away from the bloody occupation of the Philippines.

"Well, actually General, there is another matter I would like to discuss with you as well."

I love the surprise statement that tips my host back on his heels.

"What would that be, Mr. President?" The friendly, but calculating figure with a slightly high-pitched voice rejoins.

"The people of the Philippines would like to thank you for your work as part of General MacArthur's staff in preparing our country's defense against this horrendous war."

"Sir. . . " the General starts, but stops suddenly, struck with a thought that blocks more words from exiting his mouth.

As I reach into my right coat pocket, I declare, "We would like you to be honored along with the others on General MacArthur's staff, with this small token of thanks from the people of the Philippines." Slowly, I pull a check in the amount of $50,000 out of my coat, letting it flutter to a standstill in front of General Eisenhower.

"Oh, Mr. President. . . "The General is again lost for words.

Light projecting through the windows catches the white paper of the check, silhouetting my left shoulder in its reflective glow.

"Mr. President, I cannot, in good conscience or according to Army Regulations, accept this money. I truly apologize for any impression I may have given that I could."

I quickly lower the check, placing it down gently upon the table between us.

Why is this Boy Scout not taking this gift?

"General, I can assure you that President Roosevelt and Secretary Stimson have approved of this."

Silence reigns in the room. No one moves.

"Mr. President, you, and the people of the Philippines are more than generous. As a member of the Armed Services of The United States, I CANNOT TAKE THIS MONEY!"

MacArthur jumped at his check. This guy can't believe he's being honorable, can he?

"I fully understand, General," I say, as I remove the check from the table. "This has been a lovely meal. Let us have a toast to victory over Japan!"

"Yes, Mr. President . . . to victory over Japan!" General Eisenhower repeats, in a lower voice than he's used all evening.

We both down the remnants of red wine left in our glasses just as a dessert of individual fruit tarts is brought to the table by a crisply white-suited negro.

*****

President of Philippines, Manuel Quezon
https://commons.wikimedia.org/wiki/File:Manuel_L._Quezon_(November_1942).jpg

General Douglas MacArthur
https://en.wikipedia.org/wiki/Douglas_MacArthur

Major General Dwight D. Eisenhower
https://en.wikipedia.org/wiki/Dwight_D._Eisenhower

On January 3, 1942, one month into World War II for the United States and the Philippines, President Quezon of the Philippines personally gave General Douglas MacArthur $500,000 (in 1942 dollars which would be valued at $ 7,574,580.65 in 2015) out of the Philippines treasury. In addition, three staff officers of MacArthur's – Sutherland, Richard Marshall, and Huff received a total of $140,000, which would be over $2 million in 2015 dollars. At the time, MacArthur was receiving an $18,000 salary and $15,000 in allowances from the

Philippine Commonwealth in addition to a penthouse suite at the Manila Hotel and his pension as a U.S. Major General. The transfer was made with the assurance that the President of the United States and the Secretary of War had been informed. President Roosevelt was in a difficult position with MacArthur, and at the time was doing whatever he could to please him, so despite regulations, approved the gift.

On June 20, 1942, Quezon offered Lieutenant General Eisenhower a similar honorarium. Eisenhower politely but firmly declined it. Eisenhower was offered the gift because he had been a member of General MacArthur's staff in the Philippines until 1939, and in June of 1942, he had just been named commander of U.S. Army operations in Europe, his stepping stone to becoming Supreme Allied Commander Europe and eventually the President of the United States. General Eisenhower never took the money and reported the offer to his superiors.

Larrabe, Eric: *Commander In Chief: Franklin Delano Roosevelt, His Lieutenants, and Their War*, Simon and Schuster, 1987, P. 315

B-17 "Flying Fortress"
http://olive-drab.com/idphoto/id_photos_bombers_b17.php

There it is, an X marking the target!

"VISUAL CONFIRMATION OF THE TARGET, 11 O'CLOCK," the bombardier calls out on the plane's comm.

"CONFIRMED, TARGET IN SIGHT," the pilot, Bickler, calls back instantly.

Yes, I did it. My second successful night naviga-tion and this time as a temporary sit-in for the crew's nor-mal navigator. I wasn't so sure we were in the right place. Thank God, we found the training target.

Our lumbering B-17 slowly banks to the west, lining up the nose of the aircraft so that it is aimed directly in the middle of the four lights marking the desolated target area.

"WE'RE LINED UP," Bickler shouts.

"TAKING OVER," the bombardier, whose name I can't recall, replies.

Settling into a straight and level course, the plane feels like it's released from all of nature's stresses. No longer are our four supercharged turbo Curtis-Wright Cyclone engines straining to turn this mighty machine against the forces of wind and gravity. Instead, their purr reveals a comfort in place and time, as if they are taking a break, sitting down, and relaxing now that they simply have to keep the plane airborne.

"ONE AWAY," the bombardier calls out.

The engines rev up, straining to restart their laborious task, as Bickler yells, "CIRCLING FOR A SECOND PASS."

We've dropped one 100-pound training bomb, presumably on the target. Over 90 pounds of sand and four pounds of dynamite to give us a sense of what it will be like to drop a real bomb on the Nazis.

Shouldn't the wind be coming from the west? Why were the engines easing up when the plane was heading west?

"WE'RE LINED UP," Bickler shouts again.

"TAKING OVER," the bombardier calls back.

Again, the plane settles into a comfortable flight along the same path as the wind. I check my compass and readings.

We should be heading into the wind tonight.

"TWO AWAY," the bombardier gruffly barks into the comm.

Bursting back to life, the engines yank the plane east, fighting the wind as we turn for another pass.

"CIRCLING FOR A THIRD PASS," Bickler offers.

The wind is going the wrong way. Why is the wind going the wrong way? Can we be in the wrong place?

"WE'RE LINED UP;" Bickler calls out for a third time.

"TAKING OVER," the bombardier replies.

As we settle into this third bomb run, I run some numbers.

We arrived at the target 10 minutes later than I thought, but there was a headwind and almost complete pitch-blackness since leaving Dalhart. We had banked west upon getting airborne, flew at 300 miles an hour for 25 minutes, and...

"THREE AWAY," the bombardier perfunctorily calls out, as if bored by the experience.

For a fourth time, the engines begin to strain.

"CIRCLING FOR A FOURTH PASS," Bickler calls back.

"DALHART ON THE PIPE, ASKING WHERE WE ARE?" the radio operator, Goeringer, yells above the din of the engines.

Bickler yells back, "TELL THEM WE'RE OVER THE TARGET, CIRCLING FOR A FOURTH PASS."

"YES SIR," Goeringer shouts.

The airbase is asking questions. How can it be that the math doesn't add up, the airfield is concerned, but yet the target is right here?

"WE'RE LINED UP," Bickler calls out for a fourth time.

"TAKING OVER," the bombardier replies.

"DALHART SAYS SOMEONE IS DROPPING ON A TOWN!" the radio operator yells.

"FOUR AWAY," the bombardier calls out again.

Can we be bombing a town? Are there people down there?

"DALHART IS ORDERING US TO RETURN TO BASE!" Goeringer belts out.

"WORKS FOR ME," Bickler replies with a slight crackle in his voice.

There were three other bombers on our mission. Maybe one of them got lost. Maybe it was one of them accidentally bombing a town.

"GET US HOME TEMP," Bickler orders.

"YES SIR," I reply, knowing full well that I have no definitive idea where we are.

Somebody's going to be in big trouble. Could it be us?

*****

Boise City Bomb landmark in Boise City
https://owlcation.com/humanities/BoiseCityBombing

Boise City, Oklahoma, holds the distinction of being the only mainland U.S. town bombed during World War II. This event was not the result of any German, Italian, or Japanese attempt to break through U.S. defenses.

On July 5, 1943 a U.S. Air Force B-17 bomber on a training mission from Dalhart, Texas, knocked out the local Baptist church and some storage buildings over forty miles from its intended target. Navigated by a temporary navigator who was not part of the regular crew, the bomber became lost in the night. Somehow, after leaving the Dalhart base, the temporary navigator made a 45-mile mistake: he mistook the four lights centered on Boise City's main square for the intended practice target.

No casualties resulted in Boise City, but the future flight status of the pilot and crew were seriously questioned. As it turned out, this B-17 crew became one of America's most highly decorated in World War II. Not only were its members each awarded nearly a dozen medals and citations, but they also were chosen to lead 800 planes from the 8th Air Force on the first daylight bombing raid of Berlin in March 1944.

Shortly after the accidental bombing of Boise City, someone posted a sign at the base that read: "Remember the Alamo, remember Pearl Harbor, and, for God's sake, remember Boise City!" In a move that reflected the patriotic fervor of the times, the next morning, the town's mayor issued a statement praising the bomber for its accuracy. All but one bomb landed within 93 feet of the courthouse.

One crewmember even went on to marry a Boise City Girl.

The temporary navigator was assigned other duties than navigation even though an inquiry into the bombing revealed airborne night images of the city and the intended target were identical.

Flatcar

"*I*t's not your blanket," the older boy with blue eyes and chubby cheeks screams at me as he rips the soiled and worn stitched piece of comfort from my hands.

"I'm cold, give it back," I beg.

Chubby cheeks quickly steps over a girl who is lying down with her eyes shut before scrambling around two other children huddled together. He is across the car before I can even get up.

Getting up is hard. My legs are stiff. I've been sitting on my knees in the straw of this flatcar for a long time. I cannot stand up, or I will bump other kids.

There are a lot of kids with me. I thought it would be fun to take the train, but I'm not having fun. Everyone is so mean. The man at the train station yelled at us to "STAY INSIDE!"

Someone took my shoes last night when I was sleeping. Chubby cheeks just took my blanket.

A small label with my name and the word *HANOVER,* where I am to get off, is pinned to my shirt so I will not lose it. The metal rubs my skin and makes my shoulder cold.

My hands are cold.

The snow is falling on me.

I don't understand why they did not put us inside the train. Don't they know it's snowing?

I try lifting my legs to put my hands under them, but they are so hard to move.

I miss my mommy.

She put me on the train two days ago.

"Why can't you come with me?" I asked.

"Be brave. Aunt Hedda will take care of you. . . . until I. . . arrive." Mommy mumbled as she wiped tears and ash from her eyes. The explosions were very close to the train station. Every few minutes a burst would erupt somewhere nearby. We were very scared.

We had run to the train station, Mommy holding my hand, mixed with a crowd of people from our neighborhood when the explosions hit our houses. Mommy's dress was torn and singed.

We waited at the train station for a long time. Trains came and went during that time, but we could not get past the other people to get on.

After a long wait, an announcement was made that a set of flatcars were coming.

"JUST CHILDREN, NO ADULTS!"

I don't understand why Mommy could not come.

No one's mommy came.

The flatcars were quickly attached to the end of an overcrowded train covered with people hanging off of the sides and on the roof. A man pushed me away from Mommy and tossed me onto one of the flatcars. When I turned around, I could not see Mommy.

As we pulled out of the station, I looked for her, but could not find her in the crowd. I waved wildly, hoping that she might see me, but the hundreds of other kids were doing the same thing. There were so many adults, so many kids, and so much commotion.

Late last night, our flatcars disconnected from the train. We rolled for a long time as the train went away. Several kids woke up while we were rolling. Some of the bigger boys cheered as the train disappeared up the track.

Other kids sat, like I did, wondering where it was going without us.

After a while, the flatcars stopped rolling. We have been sitting in the same spot since then.

Why isn't anyone coming to get us? I wish Daddy were here. He would give me a big warm hug and rub my cold hands and feet.

I've not seen Daddy for over a year. He looked so handsome in his uniform as he climbed the stairs for his train.

Is Daddy at Aunt Hedda's house? Daddy will be at Aunt Hedda's house. Mommy will be there. And we will be warm.

The last time I went to Aunt Hedda's house was two years ago, when I was four. She lives far away from us, near Hanover. Mommy told me that she and Daddy moved to Insterburg before I was born.

I wish they had not moved. I would not have to take this train ride. I would already be in Hanover with Daddy and Mommy.

The snow is falling heavier now.

Last February, I made a snowman in front of our house. Now I am turning into a snowman.

I am so cold.

I wish Mommy were here.

"We should go find help," one of the older boys says to no one in particular.

Another of the older boys looks around at the forest we are in, asking, "Where would we go?"

I look up the line. The last town I remember passing was far away. The train had been moving for some time between that town and when our flatcar detached.

Where are we? Daddy would know where we are.

I'm hungry.

It has been a long time since I finished the stale bread, cheese, and juice Mommy packed for me. I don't think she expected the train to take this long to get to Hanover.

My legs are numb. Ice is beginning to form on my legs. I cannot straighten them.

Why can't I straighten my legs?

"I can't straighten my legs!" I yell out.

The girl who is lying down with her eyes shut next to me has ice forming over her cheeks. She will not move out of the way so I can move my legs.

No one heard me. Where is Mommy? She would warm me up.

My stomach growls at the same time that my head falls forward for an instant. I jerk it back up, keeping myself awake.

I'm tired.

Closing my eyes again, I can see Mommy and Daddy standing next to a fire at Aunt Hedda's house.

The fire is so warm.

I run to Daddy, who scoops me up into his big arms. My arms and legs are warm. Mommy gives me a kiss and hugs me from around Daddy's arms.

Don't ever put me on a train again!

"We promise we won't."

*****

Example of a flatbed railcar
https://en.wikipedia.org/wiki/Railroad_car

Flatcars carrying 142 children were separated from a train evacuating German civilians from the advancing Soviet Army in the winter of 1945. The train that they were attached to did not stop, potentially not realizing that it had lost such precious cargo or perhaps not wanting to take the chance of being attacked by aircraft if it stopped. No one knew the children were left there. They were discovered several days later. All 142 children had frozen to death.

First Line of Defense

"*G*o left… toward the water!" Erich screams out.

The steering wheel lurches, first to the left, then to the right, and then back to the left as our little Kubelwagen (bucket car) bounces and bumps over the sandy beach at over 40 kilometers per hour.

"Ok, ok," I reply, knowing that as much as I want to, I have little if any control over which way our improvised dune buggy of four drunken officers is headed. Realizing how pointless attempting to hold the steering wheel would be, I reach down with my right hand to grab the bottle of '38 Barolo Erich is guarding under his left arm.

Seeing I'm going for the wine, Erich yells out, "Hold the wheel! HOLD THE WHEEL!" He reaches out with both arms to try to stabilize the steering wheel.

The Barolo is free!

I grab the bottle quickly, just in time to save it from hitting the floor when the Kubelwagen makes a hard landing from a jump off of a sand dune.

"I can't hold it steady!" Erich yells as I press my foot to the brake and slow down the car.

Good, now I can find my bottle opener

The Kubelwagen comes to a halt on the upward slope of another sand dune.

Erich looks shaken. Sober, he is a commanding figure in his crisp Captain's uniform. Drunk, he is a nervous, disheveled mess of a child with no balls.

"That was fuck'n great!" Jürgen slurs from the back seat.

"I have next swig," Horst calls from behind me as I fumble with the bottle opener on the Barolo.

My fingers are numb from the bouncing steering wheel, slowing down my already alcohol-impaired ability to do anything requiring fine motor skills.

"Damn it, Peter, I'm thirsty!" Horst yells as he kicks my seat from behind.

"I'm opening i…."

BOOOM BOOM BOOOOM BOOOM BOOM BOOOM BOOOOM

Before I can say the word *it*, a series of explosions rock the beach, spraying sand and dirt into the Kubelwagen from all directions.

What the hell is going on?

Jürgen cheers as each new explosion sends towering geysers of debris into the sky. "Yeah, Yeah, Yeah!"

Dazed and confused, Erich looks around.

Horst calls out, "Give me the damn wine!"

Sand is blowing in every direction, as my fingers are finally able to manipulate the bottle opener. I twist to the rhythm of the explosions.

BOOM

Right twist.

BOOOOOOM

Riiiiight twist.

BOOOOM

Riiiight twist.

The cork comes out with what I can only as-sume was a pop.

BOOOOM

No sand in the bottle.

I throw the cork down with my left hand while I quickly bring the Barolo up to my mouth with my right, hitting the glass bottle on my front teeth a little too hard.

Horst kicks the seat again, yelling something I can't hear.

BOOOOM

Ahh, that's good wine.

I sit for a moment to savor the taste of the Barolo before it dawns on me; the explosions stopped. The Kubelwagen is silent for a brief instant.

"Give me the bottle!" Horst yells out, again kicking my seat.

I turn to hand the bottle behind me when out in the distance a ship – no, a *flotilla* – catches my eye.

I stare for a moment as the image of a few ships turns into many, then hundreds.

They're heading toward the beach!

I drop the Barolo toward Horst as my mind loses grip to the awesome site.

Jürgen taps me on the shoulder. "We're going to need more wine for our guests," he slurs.

"Damn it, Peter!" Horst yells out, brushing red wine off of his uniform as he turns his head toward me. "You spilled it!"

The ships are getting closer to the beach. As they do so, the front of the ship closest to us opens to reveal a ramp.

Jürgen punches my shoulder. "We'll take the ship! Drive onto the ramp!"

Without thinking, I floor the gas and turn the steering wheel. The little Kubelwagen jumps to a start as it begins clawing its way up the sand and then left toward the beach.

That's a big ship!

Erich, who has been silent since we first saw the ships, turns to me and smirks, "We're going to capture a ship." A small smile flits across his face.

The ship approaches the beach just as the Kubelwagen reaches the water line. The ramp of the open front of the ship is directly in front of me, so I press the gas pedal, and we drive our Kubelwagen right up onto the ship. Hundreds of American soldiers and a tank meet us at the top of the ramp.

One of the soldiers toward the front yells out, "What the hell are you doing?"

Jürgen replies in English "We're taking your ship."

I didn't know Jürgen spoke English.

Several of the Americans have their guns aimed at us. One, with a set of double bars on his uniform, walks toward the Kubelwagen, toward me. A slow gait to his step betrays some hesitation.

As Horst stands up in his seat, his metal belt buckle scratches the back of my head. He extends his left arm toward the American, offering him the almost-empty bottle of Barolo.

Damn it, he's wasting it!

The American takes the Barolo, puts it to his lips and, with some reluctance, takes the final swig. He smiles and then reaches into his jacket and lifts out a small flask, which he hands to Horst.

Without hesitation, Horst gulps down whatever is in the flask.

Erich turns to me and says, under his breath, "I don't think we can take this ship."

There are a lot of Americans.

Our Kubelwagen is now surrounded by Americans. One offers me his hand. I take it.

He pulls me out of the driver's seat just as Erich, Jürgen, and Horst are also removed from the little car.

Our war is over.

Jürgen asks, "What was in the flask?"

"Scotch," Horst replies.

The American with the flask smiles and leads
us away from our Kubelwagen.

*****

A German Kubelwagon

In the early morning of January 22, 1944, American and British forces conducted an amphibious invasion on the Italian coast near a small town called Anzio. The only Germans on the beach at Anzio when the Allied forces came ashore were four drunken officers in a Volkswagen Kubelwagen, who proceeded to drive up through the open doors of a LST (Landing Ship Tank).

The landing at Anzio was intended to be an Allied surprise to get behind a German defensive line. Surprise was initially achieved, but instead of taking advantage of the weak defenses on the beach, the Allies sat on their beachhead, providing the Germans with time to bring in massive reinforcements. Without the element of surprise, the Allies then endured a long siege by those German reinforcements.

Afterword

*A*ll the stories in this collection are based on real events. Since the individuals involved could not be interviewed, everything written here is fiction. The human story, as we know it, is fiction wrapped around actual events. So little can be known for sure, even by those present in the moment of the event, that attempting to come to truth is simply choosing a narrative to believe. Yet, when we weave all our stories together, we come up with something far more profound than anything we could have created alone. We come up with the rich tapestry of humanity.

This is the first of, hopefully, many collections from The 20th Century's War. I barely touched on World War I and World War II here, but there is so much more to write about that episode of The 20th Century's War. Other episodes will also include stories from Korea, Vietnam, the wars in the Balkans, the Russian Revolution, multiple conflicts in Afghanistan, and all the flare-ups in the Middle East since 1898.

Unfortunately, The 20th Century's War is not yet over. Our modern human story of wanton waste is still being written.

I sincerely hope you enjoyed reading this book as much as I enjoyed writing it. If you did, I would greatly appreciate a short review on your favorite book website. Reviews are crucial for any author, and even just a line or two can make a huge differ-ence.

http://bit.ly/2jVllaT

About the Author

Jeremy R. Strozer

*R*aised in California, Jeremy moved to the Washington, D.C. area at the age of 18 to attend university. Through education and luck, he became a Fulbright Fellow, a Presidential Management Fellow, and found ways to live and work across vast swaths of the world. Professionally, Jeremy helped remove unexploded ordnance from war-ravaged countries; stem the flow of the world's most dangerous weapons; and potentially reduced the likelihood of war between a couple of the world's most powerful countries.

He lives in Falls Church, Virginia, with his wife, son and daughter where he continues to work on preventing future war and warning the world about the human cost of violence.

If you like what you've just read, please consider following Jeremy at:

JeremyStrozer.com

https://www.facebook.com/jeremystrozerauthor/

Twitter: @jeremystrozer

Sponsor his writing and podcast on Patreon

https://www.patreon.com/jeremystrozer